UNLIKELY GUARDIAN

Uncle Chip Saves the Fae
Book 1

JAMIE DAVIS

Acknowledgments

This book made possible with the generous assistance of these Kickstarter Backers:

Kristi Preston-Barnes, Dom Graham, Jessica Spring, Martha Carr, Conrad J, Nic Anderson, Glen Errington, Christian "Mecki" Hejl, Gerald P. McDaniel, Ryan Scott James, Delia A Landstrom, Arveyah Wright, Merri, Brianna Welch-Martin, E.M. Middel, Mary Eleanor, Kathy D C, Deborah Snowden, Dr. Cindy Ann Simon, Rabbi Fred Natkin, Beth Jones, Carol Cha, Rec, Sue Byrne, Karen Johnson, Stephen Ballentine, Melinda Kucsera, Scott McConnell Distance CME, Sabrina Graham, Nan & Rick W., Jenn Mitchell, Renee Roberts

Rose

I dove to the side just in time to avoid the hammer blow of the demon's descending fist. This guardian spirit had been summoned more than a millennia ago to watch over the resting place of my current quest, the Star of Azothine. I'd been working at this dig location in central Iraq off and on for three years to uncover the hidden temple. Word had come two days ago they were close to finding the hidden temple.

The demon recovered faster than I expected, coalescing into its full corporeal form. Deep crimson scales covered it from head to toe. It stood upright, its horned head reaching the ceiling nearly fifteen feet above the floor.

A clawed finger pointed at me as I rolled back to my feet. "You defile this place, Woman. Know that others will defile you and yours."

What a strange thing to say. I took several steps to the left as I tried to circle around closer to the altar behind the demon. "I came for the Star of Azothine. Let me have it and you may go back to your eternal rest."

A loud, bellowing laugh was the only response I got. The demon charged at me; arms outstretched to crush me in a clawed embrace.

I realized I'd moved into a corner which gave me few avenues to escape past the massive arms. My only option was to run straight at the temple guardian.

The move caught it by surprise. The creature stumbled a little in an effort to slow his advance and bring his arms in faster to catch me.

I slashed to the right and then back to the left before dropping to my knees and laying backward to slide between the demon's stubby legs. The smooth flagstone floor aided my escape.

Rage filled the roar from the demon. It stomped its cloven hooves on the floor in an attempt to crush me beneath them.

I rolled to the right until I came up against the altar that held the object of my quest. There was no time to admire the large star sapphire set into the stone carvings adorning the front of the stone table. The demon had twisted around and raked a clawed hand at me.

"Uhnnn," I grunted as one of the claws pierced my body armor. Fiery pain lanced through my side where the claw dug into my ribs.

I spun away, avoiding the grasping hand trying to close around me. My sword scored a deep slash down through the guardian's wrist. The magical silver blade was the only weapon in my arsenal that could touch the creature.

The altar at my back, I twisted, and half climbed, half leaped to stand on the ceremonial table. It brought me eye to eye with the demon.

"Defiler, you will pay for corrupting this unholy place with your presence."

"Yeah, yeah, why don't you stop complaining and do something about it."

The demon let out another angry roar that shook the pillars holding the ancient roof in place. Dust and bits of stone dropped from above. It ignored the impending collapse, instead charging at me once again.

This time I waited for the demon to come to me while I called upon my Fae magic to infuse the sword with even more energy.

When the guardian spread its scaly arms to strike at me, I dashed off the altar, leaping high enough to pass over the demon's shoulder. As I passed, I stabbed deep into the creature's neck, piercing the scaly hide with ease.

The howl that erupted turned quickly into a gurgling cough as black ichor fountained from its mouth.

I slid down the demon's back, landing on the floor behind it.

Clawed hands clutched at its throat as more of the demonic blood spurted from the open wound I'd left in passing. It fell to its knees where it wobbled a little before falling over onto its side.

I watched it for several seconds to be sure it wasn't going to rise again, then marched past the guardian's corpse to stand in front of Azothine's altar. I wiped my sword blade on a rag from my pocket then sheathed it.

The gem set in the altar called to me. I had spent so long tracking this artifact down and now I had found it. All of that garbage about the curse upon those who found it now set aside. I'd performed the necessary rituals to dispel the curse and wash any effect from me. That should be enough.

I knelt and pulled my camp knife from my belt. Using the tip, I carefully pried the gemstone free until it fell into my outstretched palm. It nearly filled my hand. This would be an excellent addition to the museum foundation my family had set up long ago.

The gemstone slid easily into my pocket as I turned to make my way back out through the narrow gap in the cavern discovered beneath the dig site. As I crawled out on my hands and knees, I remembered the strange pronouncement from the demon during the fight. What had the guardian meant by others defiling mine. My what?

I reached the surface, emerging from the tunnel inside the white tent erected to ward off the scorching Iraqi sun high above. My dig master stood waiting for me. He was loyal to me and my family, as his family had been for centuries before.

"It's good to see you made it back, Rose."

"Do I detect a hint of doubt I would return, Taren?"

"Why, because you foolishly opted to enter without any backup?"

"I was the only one who had been cleansed of the curse from the temple's guardian."

"Well, you survived, so it's a moot point." He picked up a small metal box with a velvet-lined interior.

I dug the gem from my pocket and dropped it inside. When it

landed in the cushioned center of the box, it flashed blue as it settled into the cushioned interior.

Taren's eyebrows shot up. "Did you—?"

"I did. It's nothing. I dispelled any potential magical harm before entering."

"You think you did."

I shook my head. "I'm a powerful enough spell caster to have detected anything that might have eluded my protections."

He closed the box, which clicked as the simple locking mechanism engaged. "I'll put this with the other things you want forwarded to the museum for exhibit?"

"Yes. It should be the center of the new collection in London."

A soft buzzing sound came from the table at the far side of the room.

Taren smirked. "That's your personal phone. It's been buzzing off and on like that since you went inside."

"You didn't answer it, did you?"

"No, your instructions to leave your things alone were perfectly clear."

I nodded. "Good. Take the box to the truck. They're packing it to go to the airport today."

"As you wish." Taren bowed and left the tent.

The phone buzzed again with an incoming call. I went over and pulled it from my shoulder bag laying on the table. The screen read "Allura."

If my aunt was calling, it couldn't be good news. I swiped to open the call and turned it on speaker so I could get out of my body armor and inspect my injuries from the fight.

"Yes, Aunty, what is it?"

"Rose, you need to return to the States right away."

"Why?" The anxious tone worried me. Allura was never fazed by anything.

"It's your sister."

"What's happened to Lili? Is she okay?"

"Rose, she's dead. So is Bobby. They died in a car accident last night. I just received notification from the authorities since they couldn't reach you."

I crumpled into the camp chair beside the table, trying to wrap my head around the news. Lili was dead, along with her husband. How? Immediately another question occurred to me.

"Are we, are we sure it was an accident?"

"That's what the human police are saying, but you know my thoughts about such things. You need to come home and look into it."

"Who's taking care of the children? Has someone told Sadie yet?"

"No, she's just four. I told her that her parents are away for a while."

My heart sank. Sadie and her little brother Addison were orphans now. My older sister and her human husband were gone forever. I wiped at the tears filling my eyes.

"I'll catch the first flight back. I can be there in twenty-four hours." I paused while I ticked off the items the family needed to do. "Has anyone contacted the brother?"

"I left a message with Chip's answering service," Allura said, referring to Bobby's jet-setting elder sibling. "They assured me he'd get the message."

"I will want to talk with you about him. I know Lili and Bobby had plans for him should something like this happen, but—"

"That is a matter for the Counselor when the last wishes in the will are formally read. I will not entertain any interference from you, Rose. Lili was the senior of the two of you and it pertains to her children. She and her husband have the final say."

Allura's voice had a tone of finality I recognized. She wouldn't accept any further discussion on the subject.

"I'll send you my flight details as soon as I have them arranged. Can someone pick me up at the airport in Baltimore?"

"I'll see that a car is sent for you."

"Then I'll see you when I get back. Take good care of Sadie and Addison until I get there."

"I will always protect the future Fae queen, Rose. That has been our family's purpose for almost five hundred years."

Allura hung up the phone on her end, cutting off the call. I sat there staring at the blank screen for several minutes before I shook myself and pulled my sleeve down over my hand to wipe at the tears streaming down my face. There would be a time to mourn my older sister. First, I intended to find out if this was truly an accident or not. My thoughts went back to what the temple guardian had said during our fight. Had something defiled me and mine, as in my sister and her husband?

The answer lay in a small town in the center of Maryland. I intended to find out.

2

Chip

I pulled my Tesla to the curb in front of the unassuming two-story home. The normally quiet cul-de-sac had filled with vehicles today as the funeral goers returned to the family's home following the graveside ceremony.

Mia, my girlfriend, tapped me on the arm as I stopped. "You don't have to be all brave with me, Chip Proctor. It's okay to let your walls down when we're alone."

"I suppose you want me to cry and let it all out."

"If that's what you feel inside, then yes, that's exactly what I want you to do."

I turned in my seat to face her. Damn, she was hot, even in the plain black dress she'd selected for today. Of course, hot was what supermodels did, even at somber moments like this one. "Mia, I can't let this get to me right now. You know everything I have going on. I'm in the middle of the biggest mutual fund release of my career. If I let Bobby and Lili's deaths in a fiery crash pull my attention away, even a little bit, I could miss a detail that would put the whole deal at risk."

"That's what you have a partner for. Eddie can handle it. You always say, 'Eddie can handle anything,' so let him deal with it for a few days. The final release isn't for a month or so anyway. You know he'd agree with me. I'll bet he even told you exactly that."

I stared past Mia through the window at the mourners walking into the front door of what had been his little brother's home. The service at the funeral home had been packed with friends from the community as well as the expected family members from both sides.

"I need to get inside. I have to check on the kids, Sadie especially. She's old enough for this to scar her if we're not careful." At four, my niece was asking awkward questions of the adults around her about when she'd see her parents again. The heart-wrenching anguish of having to tell her each time that her mommy and daddy weren't coming back, that they were in heaven, still ached inside. My nephew, Addison, at almost six months old, was lucky enough to be mostly oblivious to the loss.

"Go, be with them," Mia said. "I'll be right there, nearby if you need me. I have to check in with the agency to make sure they've cleared my photo shoots for the next few days. I think we should stay here a bit longer than we'd planned."

"You're the best, Mia. I don't know how I would've gotten through this without you by my side."

"I'm not the heartless supermodel they make me out to be in all the tabloids, darling, at least not with those I love."

I smiled and popped open the door to head inside. As I got out, I spotted the candy-apple red restored Pontiac Firebird parked in the driveway. A twinge of annoyance pulled at my attention. Rose had gotten back first from the graveside. She'd been staying with the kids since the accident. I shouldn't be angry about Lili's sister stepping in to care for the little ones, but something about it struck me as wrong. I don't know why it bothered me. It wasn't like I'd ever been the type to settle down and have kids. That had always been Bobby's path in life. He took to it like a fish to water, which made me the perfect rich uncle, who visited often and spoiled the kids rotten.

I shook off the feeling of wrongness. Despite our history, I wouldn't let Rose get under my skin today. She was the better option to care for the kids despite her usual penchant for traveling the globe to dangerous places on her archeological expeditions. If she had stepped in to take over full time, I should be glad the kids had family there to watch over them. I had to be strong for Sadie and Addison, and that included not letting Aunt Rosie push my buttons.

As I approached the house across the freshly cut grass of the front lawn, a strange sensation tugged at the awareness at the back of my mind. It was like I knew what the kids, especially Sadie, were doing and feeling at any given moment. I'd been having these feelings for days now, ever since the accident. Right now, I had a vision of Sadie crying alone in a room full of adults who could do nothing to soothe her pain.

She needed me.

I picked up speed and burst through the front door, my head swiveling as I searched for my niece. I spotted her sitting on a chair placed in front of a wooden snack tray. A paper plate with a half a ham and cheese sandwich and a dollop of macaroni salad on it sat in front of her. She hadn't touched the food. Her eyes searched among all the faces around her, adults in conversation with each other and paying no attention to the sad little girl in their midst. Her big, wide eyes brimmed with tears.

In an instant, I found myself down on one knee next to her, my voice taking on a bad British accent. "My lovely Princess Sadie, your loyal knight Sir Chip is here to deal with any who would do you harm. Tell me where the dragon is, and I'll slay it."

Her sad eyes brightened, and she flung herself from the chair, wrapping her small arms around my neck. She squeezed with surprising strength for a little girl. I worried she'd started crying all over again until I heard a light giggle escape her. She let go and settled on my knee.

"Uncle Chip, you're silly. There are no dragons here."

I gave her a wide-eyed expression of shock. "No? Well, that's because you don't know where to look. Dragons can disguise themselves, you know. Why, any of these people could be monsters of one sort or another. Let me stay close and protect you while you eat your lunch."

Sadie giggled again and slid off my knee to climb back into her chair. She took a bite of her sandwich and pointed across the room. "There's a monster, Uncle Chip. Protect me."

I glanced toward the door, following her pointing finger. Mia had just entered. "Surely not Aunty Mia? She's the nicest lady in the whole world."

Sadie shrugged and picked up her cup to drink some milk, her four-year-old mind already distracted and on to something else.

I marveled at how easily she was able to shift her mind away from things. It must be something all kids were able to do. I wondered where it went by the time people became adults. Being able to forget, even for a moment, would've come in handy at times like this.

Lost in my thoughts, I didn't hear Rose walk up behind me.

"Sadie, dear, don't let your uncle distract you from eating your lunch. You haven't eaten a thing all day, and I don't want you telling me you have a tummy ache later on."

"Yes, Aunt Rose. See, I took bites already." Sadie held up her sandwich to display how much she'd eaten.

"Well, good. Keep it up. You want to grow up big and strong like me, don't you?"

Sadie nodded and took another bite, washing it down with more milk from her cup.

I stood and leaned close to Rose. I inhaled a whiff of her sweet perfume as I said, "She wasn't eating anything and looked like she was about to cry when I came in, Rose. I was just trying to distract her from her sad thoughts so she could eat something. Is that so bad?"

"She's been through a lot, Chip. All these people here are disrupting her day even more. Soon they'll all be gone, and then she'll be all alone to go to bed and try to understand why her mommy and daddy aren't there to sing her to sleep."

I felt the same strange ire I'd experienced outside in the car at the thought of anyone but me taking care of the two kids. I tamped it down once again. "Look, Rose, I know you've been here since everything happened and have stepped in to take care of Sadie and Addison. I know everyone in the family is thankful for that. But don't take it out on us that you have to do it. I know it's been hard."

"No, Chip, you don't. That's the point. You got the news and put off coming down here until last night. Your latest business venture couldn't be put on hold, I suppose. Now you're here and you want to tell me what to do when I've been the one who's been here doing what was needed the whole time."

I held up a hand. "You're right. I'm sorry. You've done so much. I know you and Lili were as close as Bobby and I were. Can we declare a truce for the next day or so? Honest. I don't want to fight with anyone. I just want what's best for them." I glanced down at Sadie who sat carefully stabbing a piece of macaroni with her plastic fork before shoving it into her mouth. She didn't need to see her two closest remaining adult relatives bickering at a time like this.

"Where's Addison?" I checked around the room, expecting to see someone holding him.

Rose nodded toward the stairs. "He's up in his room, down for a nap. At least he's keeping to his usual schedule pretty well, despite all this mess."

I smiled. "At least one member of the family is sleeping well."

Rose's mouth quirked up in a half smile of her own. "The gods will always bless the little ones at times like this."

I let her strange turn of phrase pass by. I knew their family wasn't particularly religious, but I'd never looked into what they believed. I didn't really care. It wasn't like I was up to evangelizing anyone. I hadn't set foot in a church since I was a teenager. I still remembered the fight with my mom and dad about being old enough to choose my own spiritual path.

As if on cue, both my parents walked up at that moment.

"That was such a lovely tribute to your brother at the funeral home, Chip," my mother said, pulling me close for a one-armed hug while she held her plastic cup in the other. I wondered if she'd raided Bobby's liquor cabinet to spike her iced tea or if she was drinking it straight for once. I couldn't detect any alcohol on her, but that didn't mean anything. She'd always been good at hiding that part of her life as a mostly functional alcoholic.

"Thanks, Mom. I only said what was true. Bobby had it all, the perfect wife, family, and kids. It was too sad it all had to end so suddenly."

My father clapped a hand on my shoulder and gave it a squeeze. "She's right, son. What you said set the tone for the service. I guess I should say you both did." He smiled and reached out to take Rose's hand as well. "Your words about Lili said so much about how much you looked up to your big sister, Rose."

"Thank you, Mr. Proctor. It's hard to know what to say at a time like this. I hope I was able to memorialize her in a way that did her justice."

"I think everyone here would say you did," my father said. "And please, remember to call us Chuck and Nancy. We're all family after all, especially at a time like this."

"Yes, dear," my mother added. "By the way, has there been any word about a will or who will look after the children? Surely, they left some instructions on who they'll live with now."

Rose stiffened a little at the question. "It's not been determined for sure that I know of. I think there is supposed to be a Counselor around later this afternoon to dispose of at least some of that."

"Well, Chuck and I want to throw our hats into the ring. We would love to be the ones to raise the two of them if no one else is available. I mean, your parents are dead as well, Rose, and you have your career."

"No."

My eyebrows shot up in surprise as both Rose and I echoed the same response to the suggestion simultaneously. While my parents wouldn't do anything to overtly harm the kids, they were getting older and both had underlying health issues, not to mention my mother's drinking problem.

"I'd assumed Rose would be taking on the job," I said. "I mean, she's been here since the accident and the kids seem to love her." Even as I said it, something about it felt off to me. It left a bad taste in the back of my mouth. I pushed past the odd feeling and put on a smile of support for my sister-in-law.

Rose returned my smile. "Thank you, Chip. I hope I'll have your support when the Counselor arrives. I'm unsure how things will shake out."

A tug on the sleeve of my sportscoat pulled me away from the conversation. Sadie stood at my side again.

"Uncle Chip, can you come out back and push me on the swing?"

"Sure, kiddo. I was finished talking with Gram, Pop, and Aunt Rose anyway." I let her lead me away from the others and walked out into the yard to play in the fresh air and sunshine. Maybe I'd forget about the events of the morning for a little while.

3

Rose

I watched as Chip took Sadie by the hand to go out to the back yard. As I stood there, I realized I'd started grinding my teeth and forced myself to relax.

"Has anyone told him what's about to happen yet?"

I turned, recognizing the voice that sounded like a metal box dragged across a gravel parking lot. "Hello, Warren. I've been trying to reach you for two days now."

The werewolf and part-time private investigator put on something approaching a sympathetic smile across his bearded face. "I had other business out of town to attend to. I came back as soon as I could after I heard about your sister and Bobby. I figured your family would want all available resources on deck. So sorry about what happened, Rose. Has anyone taken up the investigation yet?"

"The human investigators called it a tragic car accident, but they wouldn't be looking for the same things we would. This is one of those times I'm glad most of them are blind to the magical world around them. And the answer is no. We have not assigned another investigator. Aunt Allura has allowed me, as the arms mistress, to lead that effort."

"And you were waiting for me? I'm flattered."

"Don't be. No one else wants the case. They all know it has to be a deliberate attack on the family, and they don't want to get caught up in another Fae civil war of succession."

"Does that make me loyal or just plain stupid?" He let out a grunting chuckle. "Don't answer that. I know what you think of me most of the time. I'll take a look at the police report and check the vehicle for magical residue. Anything else I should know about?"

I grimaced. "No. There won't be much there when you get to the junkyard. Whatever happened out there to them set the SUV ablaze. There wasn't much but a metal frame and engine block left. We aren't even sure all the ashes we buried today are from the bodies."

Warren reached out and placed a gentle hand on my forearm. "I'm sorry, Rose. I truly am. They were good people."

I stared down at the hairy-knuckled hand on my arm until he removed it. He promptly shoved the offending member in the pocket of his slacks. "Uh, look, I didn't mean anything by that. I know you and I don't have that kind of history. You have my sympathy. It's just a tragedy, that's all."

I decided to ignore the inappropriate sign of concern. He knew better than to touch me and he wouldn't do it again. There were protocols for members of the royal family, even though we were in hiding. Instead, I turned my attention back to watching Chip through the rear family room window. He pushed Sadie on her swing out back. The look of pure joy on her face made my heart ache. "That tragedy, Warren, is exactly why we have to figure out who's behind the attack, and soon. They're bound to come after the kids next. They're especially vulnerable during this transition period until the new Guardian settles into their powers."

"Which brings me back to my original question." Warren moved around to interrupt my view of the yard. "When are you going to tell Chip about what he must do?"

"That's up to my aunt and the royal Counselor. I'm still hoping Lili changed her mind at the last minute and came to her senses. We'll see when they read the documents this afternoon."

"I thought you tested him for this. Isn't that why your sister asked you to check him out before Sadie was born?"

"It is. And I haven't changed my opinion that Chip cheated on that test, somehow."

Warren laughed. "You administered the test. How'd he manage that with you watching him?"

"I don't know," I snapped back at him. Angry at losing my temper, I shifted to the side, restoring my view of the back yard. The warrior in me wanted to make sure I knew where Sadie was at all times and who was with her. Chip's latest glamor-queen girlfriend, Mia something or other, had joined them by the swingset. "Do me a favor. While you're checking into the accident, spend a little time on Chip and what he's been up to lately. I still think he's completely unsuitable to fill this role. Maybe if we can dig up enough dirt, Allura will overrule the will."

"I wouldn't bank on that happening anytime soon. Your aunt's always been a stickler for following the letter of the law, especially when it came to the royal family and lines of succession."

"Do it anyway. Don't worry, you'll be paid your usual rate."

"What if you don't like the results? If there was something shady about your brother-in-law, you'd have sniffed it out a long time ago."

"You'll get paid either way. Just give it your due diligence once you've looked into the crash."

Warren nodded. When I kept my gaze on the little girl outside and didn't say anything more, he took the hint and drifted off towards the deli platter and collection of casseroles on the table in the dining room. I didn't begrudge him a free meal. He had taken the time to come see me and pay his respects. There were so few in the Unusual community around Westminster that did that anymore. Just because the family had come here to keep a low profile didn't mean that certain local leadership couldn't be courteous to the Fae royal family in exile.

I shook my head, my brunette shoulder-length curls bouncing a little beside my ears. Lili had always been so much better at this part of the role than I had. She'd learned at an early age how to impress the right people and build bridges rather than burning them down. I tended to be a fight first and ask for allies later type of person.

I watched as Mia took over pushing Sadie on the swing. The two were chatting about something that had the little girl smiling and engaged. Damn it, this wasn't fair. I wasn't the one who was supposed to raise the next Fae queen, Lili was. She'd reveled in the challenge and welcomed it. Now she was gone. I was all Sadie had left, other than her human Uncle Chip, that is.

A slight commotion behind me at the front door drew my attention away from Sadie again. A few people clustered around someone who'd just entered. One of them bobbed their head in a bow and one woman curtsied in an archaic and unusual show of respect when out in public like this where normal humans were around. It had to be the arrival of my Aunt Allura. She insisted on the proper protocols from the supernatural community and most people obliged her. Indulged her was more like it.

The matriarch of the family, my mother's younger sister pushed through the cluster of fawning funeral goers by the door and searched the room until her eyes fell on me. I noticed them narrow a little and then she jerked her head in a way that left no doubt in the command it carried. She stood off to the side in a black satin dress with a matching pillbox hat that had a black lace veil hanging down to the tip of her nose. The lace was thin enough such that her stern eyes were still plainly visible to all who looked her way. Allura's toe started tapping almost immediately, typically impatient when her requests weren't fulfilled immediately.

Hurrying over to her, I nodded a slight bow, ignoring the slight frown at my minimal deference. "Aunt Allura, I saw you at the graveside, but you left before I could come see you."

"I had some business to attend to on my way here." She waved her hand at the surrounding house and sniffed to show her disapproval at the lifestyle Lili and Bobby had chosen for their home. "Where is the brother? The Counselor will be here presently with the documents and talisman."

I nodded towards the rear of the house. "He's out back with Sadie at the moment. That's a good thing because I wanted to talk with you—"

"I will not go against your sister's wishes in this matter, Rose Aldreth Eldersdottir. Our family has followed the strict protocols regarding our charge to carry on the royal lineage for almost five hundred years. Now that the time is near to crown a new queen, you will not destroy that legacy because of your own foolish pride. Why weren't you here when Lilian was killed? That was your opportunity to do your duty and you failed it."

I tried to keep my eyes from widening even though the heat rushing to my face revealed my anger. She'd said it all aloud for everyone in earshot to hear. The cluster of fawning mourners by the door gasped, then began whispering amongst themselves.

Gritting my teeth and forcing a half-smile on my face, I said, "Aunt Allura, you know as well as I that following up the lead on that artifact in Iraq had been important. It could have proven dangerous if someone unprepared had found it before I did."

"But that's always your excuse, isn't it?" Allura sighed and reached up to lift the black lace from in front of her eyes, folding it back across the top of her hat. She lowered her voice and said, "Rose, I know it wasn't your fault. In hindsight it's obvious the reports were a lure to get you away from your sister so this attack would succeed. But it's all about appearances, my dear. Appearances are that you ran off to fight a demon over an archaic gemstone rather than stay and do your duty. Now we must show that we understand that duty even more. The people who support the family must have faith that we will follow the old ways and customs so that the new queen will take her place and restore the Fae to their rightful place at the head of the Unusual community."

The old woman wasn't wrong, at least in how it all looked. Didn't she know I was painfully aware of all that? I'd take it all back, give up my powers and more if I could make it so that Lili and Bobby hadn't gone out for that drive. No one even knew what they were doing out on that back country road alone in the middle of the night. They'd left the children alone at home when they did it. Why? None of it made sense.

The mystery of it all caused me to glance across the room to where Warren stood with a heaping plate of food. Even though he was across the crowded room, I knew his enhanced werewolf hearing could make out everything Allura had said. His eyes met mine and he gave a quick nod. He knew I was counting on him to find out who was behind all this. He set the plate down on the credenza, took the overstuffed sandwich from his plate, wrapped it in a napkin and headed for the front door.

Good, he'd taken the hint and started doing what he was being paid for. His exit wasn't lost on my aunt.

"You hired that wolf shifter to track the killer? Are you sure he's up to the task?"

"He'll do what needs to be done. All he has to do is identify them. I'll take care of the hard part."

"You can't just kill them, Rose. You must make sure you know who sent them and why."

"I know why. They came to kill Lili."

"Yes, but why didn't they come for the children as well? There's more going on here than we understand. That is why, when the Counselor arrives, you will do everything according to protocol and your sister's wishes. I want no interruptions that would sow doubt in the Guardian's mind about what must be done. It will be hard enough to get him to take on the task before him."

"I'll do what is necessary, Aunt Allura."

I knew the vagueness of my statement wasn't lost on her. But she didn't press the issue. The front door opened and the crowd in the entry foyer spread apart to allow a short, squat man with a long gray beard and shiny bald head walk into the living room. His head swiveled from side to side until his eyes settled on Allura and me. The gnomish attorney lifted up a brown leather briefcase and looked around the room.

Allura gestured down the hallway by the stairs and started that way herself. "Go and fetch the brother. It's time we got this over with."

She continued with the Counselor towards the study, leaving me to go get Chip in from the yard. I took a deep breath and headed out to do my duty. I could kill a four-hundred-pound tarantula demon with nothing but a battle axe. What did I have to fear from a New York stock fund manager?

Not. A. Thing.

4

Chip

"Sadie, sweetie, why don't you go and show me how you go down the slide. I think you've had enough time on the swing, okay?"

"Okay, Uncle Chip."

I helped Sadie hop down from the swing and she scampered over to the wooden castle attached to the swingset. She climbed up the ladder and I turned to Mia. "I know you said we should stay a few days, but I think we won't have to stay too much longer. It's a long drive back to New York, and I want to get in early enough to review the new prospectus for our fund before bedtime."

Mia ran a manicured finger in a light caress along my forearm. "I bet I can convince you to come to bed early."

I was about to answer her, but instead I let out an involuntary "Owww" as a sharp pain in my hand caused me to gasp and rub at my palm. At the same instant, Sadie started crying at the top of the slide on the castle's upper platform.

"Sadie, what is it?" I rushed over to her, ignoring the fading pain in my hand.

She held up her left hand. "I have an owie, Uncle Chip."

Her hand was right at my eye level, and I leaned forward to look at it. She had a small splinter of wood from the castle platform in her palm.

"Oh no, you have a little splinter there. Let me take a look at it."

She looked at me, wide-eyed with new tears forming in her eyes. "Make it better."

"I will. Give me just a second and I'll pull it out."

She tried to jerk her hand away. "That will hurt, Uncle Chip."

"No, sweetie, I promise as soon as I pull it out, it'll feel better right away. We can't leave it in there."

I dug in my pocket with my free hand while I held on to her little wrist in my other. My limited edition Swiss army knife had a small set of tweezers in the case. I should be able to make short work of this.

Sadie's tears flowed more freely as she started sobbing. "I want Mommy. Where is she? Tell her to come back, Uncle Chip."

I choked back a sob of my own as I heard her pleas. "I'm sorry, Sadie. Your Mommy had to go away. But I'm here and I'll take care of this just like she would."

Sadie's tears didn't stop flowing, but she stopped calling for her mother at least. Blinking away a few tears of my own, I positioned the tweezers carefully. I only wanted to do this once. After all, I'd promised it would feel better right away and I was a man of my word.

"Sadie, when something like this happens, you have to remember to trust that the people who love you will always be there to take care of it, understand?"

She nodded, the tears slowing a little.

"Okay, let's count to three together."

Her little voice joined mine.

"One, Two, Three."

With a flick of my fingers, I pulled the splinter from her hand.

"See, all done."

Sadie nodded and held up her hand to look at the small red spot in the center of her palm. "It still hurts."

"We'll go and wash it with some cool water and put a small bandage on it. I'm sure you know where they're kept, right?"

She nodded and leaned forward to clutch me around the neck as I lifted her from the play castle's parapet. As she leaned her head on my shoulder on one side, Mia leaned forward to whisper in my ear on the other.

"That was the hottest thing I've ever seen you do. Hurry and find that Band-Aid so we can find someplace to be alone."

I caught the playful wink she gave me followed by a swat to my butt.

"Come on Sadie, let's find those bandages, then you can play with someone else while Uncle Chip attends to some important business."

"What kind of business would that be, Uncle Chip?" Rose asked from a few feet away.

I hadn't even heard her come from the house. She had a way about her that always seemed to sneak up on you. I guess that was one of the reasons I'd seduced her at Lili and Bobby's wedding reception. I had to see what all that lithe stealthiness hid beneath the surface.

As I caught myself scanning her in the tight black dress once more, she shook her head. I realized she'd caught me at it. Her disapproving smirk said it all. Looks like she remembered that interlude during her sister's reception, too.

"What happened to Sadie?"

"Nothing to worry about, Aunt Rose," I said. "She got a splinter, but I took care of it. Now we're off to find a bandage."

"Perhaps your friend can take care of that for the moment? Then Sadie can play with her friends inside. One of the neighborhood moms stopped by with another casserole and she brought her kids with her. Sadie can hang with them while you come with me. There's some family business to attend to."

"What kind of family business?"

"My aunt has arrived with the Counselor. He's got some paperwork for us to look over."

The last thing I wanted today was to go over my brother's will or other family business. "Isn't that something that could wait a few days? I can conference in from New York."

"No, it must be done today. It's overdue already."

Her eyes flashed, which must have been a trick of the sunlight reflecting in them. I felt a sort of mental tug at my memory, then it passed. Rose's eyebrows lowered and her mouth opened to say more.

I held up a hand to stop her. "Fine, if it'll keep the family happy, I'll do it today. I still think it could wait until another time, but since your aunt went to the trouble of bringing the lawyer here today, let's get it over with."

I leaned over to Mia and shifted Sadie in her direction. "Mia, babe, be a love and take her in to get a bandage and to play with her friends. I'm sure the other mom in there knows where Lili kept things."

"Certainly, but don't be too long." She held my gaze for a long time before she carried Sadie inside.

"Wow," Rose said. "She's pretty obvious with the way she undresses you with her eyes."

"Jealous? You had your turn already. Did you want another shot?"

"Not even a little. Now come on. The Counselor is an important person and shouldn't be kept waiting too long. He has other, uh, clients to attend to."

"After you." I extended my arm and followed behind, allowing myself to appreciate her dress once again.

"Eyes level, if you don't mind."

I laughed at her understanding of exactly what I'd been doing as we walked into the house. If she wasn't such a ball-buster, there might have been a chance for us.

Rose led me through the living room and dining room before turning down the long hallway beside the stairs. I remembered Bobby and Lili had a study back here with their personal desks. It was probably the best place for a meeting like this one.

I entered behind Rose. I recognized the stern-faced woman as Lili and Rose's Aunt Allura. She was the matriarch of the family since their parents were long passed. The other person in the room had to be the oddest person I'd ever seen. He couldn't be more than four and half feet tall. He had a bald head and a long grey beard and mustache. He had spectacles pinching across the bridge of his nose and his eyes peered up at me through them, watching me the whole time I walked in.

"You must be the family lawyer." I extended a hand. "I'm Chip Proctor."

"I'm the Counselor."

He didn't take my offered hand, so I dropped it back to my side. Something about his piercing black eyes sent a shiver down my spine, and I decided to get this over with as soon as possible.

"I have to be leaving for New York soon, so can we hurry this up?"

The Counselor glanced up at Allura. "What is he talking about? He acts like he doesn't know his role in all of this."

Rose laughed, though there was no mirth in her eyes. "Oh, he doesn't. He never paid much attention to what his brother and sister-in-law were up to. It doesn't surprise me that he's oblivious to the obvious."

"What are you talking about? I came down here to visit every time they invited me and dropped in by surprise a few times to boot. I knew my brother and his wife very well."

The small man pointed to Rose. "You administered the test. We have the blood sealing his place as the Guardian to prove it."

"Yes, well, I didn't see any reason to leave him clued into the hidden realm, so I cast a glamour on him."

Allura shook her head. "You shouldn't have done that, Rose. It will only make all of this that much more difficult."

"I still held out hope my sister would come to her senses and appoint another in his place."

"And yet, she did not do so." Allura's hard eyes glared at Rose. "When had your sister ever changed her mind once she'd decided something?"

Rose squirmed a little as she answered. "There's always a first time." She pointed at Chip. "Besides, he's completely unsuited to this role."

I stepped forward, trying to wrap my head around my place in the conversation. I held up a hand interrupting the others. "I'm sorry. I'm standing right here. What test? What hidden world, for that matter? And where did you get my blood?"

"Remove the glamour, Rose," Allura said. "You set it in place so it must be you."

Rose let out a disgusted groan. She moved to stand directly in front of me. She raised her hand over my head, and I flinched a little.

"Relax, you baby. I'm not going to hurt you."

"I know that." I let out the breath I'd been holding and met her eyes with a level gaze and tried out my best bravado. "What are you going to do, cast a spell on me or something?"

"No, silly. Remove one. Now hold still."

Her hand hovered a few inches above my forehead, and I resisted the urge to stare up at it, holding my eyes on her striking green ones. They flashed again, brighter somehow, like they had outside, only this time there was no sun to cause the glow. She muttered a word I didn't know in a language I didn't understand.

A white-hot flash of light washed across me. It wasn't in the study, though. The room was as shadowed as it had been when I walked in. This was inside my mind. As it faded, a few distant memories from five years before drifted up to the surface, like a corpse floating up to bob in a river current.

"Werewolves, and magic. They're all real. You tricked me into that biker bar and…" I stopped trying to wrap my head around it all. "That was the test you're all talking about? You tried to get me killed."

Rose laughed. "You were never in any real danger. Besides, you passed the test, even though I was sure you wouldn't."

I rubbed at my right palm with my thumb. "You cut me and took a drop of my blood. I remember it all now. How did you do that?"

"Magic, Chip. Werewolves, supernatural creatures of all kinds, and magic, they're all real. Now you know the truth of the world around you because you're about to be let in on this family's greatest secret and you have to be aware of everything, so pay attention."

I glanced at Allura and the Counselor guy standing off to one side. I pointed to the shorter of the two. "And him?"

"He's a Gnome," Rose said. "They make the best Counselors in matters like this because they're immune to most magical suggestion. That makes them trustworthy witnesses to legal actions."

"So, what are you, a witch? That wouldn't surprise me, I guess."

"Oh, goodness, no. Witches and warlocks are humans who can use magic. Our family is Fae, a type of fairy, I guess you'd call it, though we're not a variety with wings and such."

Allura interrupted. "We are not anything like fairies, Rose. Do not dumb it down for him. He must come into this with his eyes open, or the Guardianship will not take hold."

"Yes, ma'am." Chastised, Rose returned her attention to him. "Chip, it's like this. Lili and I, along with Aunt Allura here, are part of a line of Royal Fae dating back several millennia. Our family has sort of been in hiding for the last four hundred and eighty-odd years waiting for the next great Fae queen to be born. That has now happened."

Allura said, "Our family has been entrusted with this duty for centuries, Charles."

I winced as she used my given name. I hated my given name.

"We had hoped to help the queen grow into her ascendancy without incident, but our cause has been revealed to some who would seek to harm the family. That is what has brought us to this moment."

I stared at the old woman, trying to process everything she and Rose had just said. My returned memories from five years ago combined together with what they'd just revealed to me in a rush of awareness. I struggled to put it all into some semblance of order in my mind. As I did, something Allura had said struck me.

"Wait a minute. You said someone tried to harm the family. That means you think Bobby and Lili's wreck wasn't an accident at all."

Rose shook her head.

Allura said, "Almost assuredly not, though we're looking into proving our suspicions to be positive."

I looked back at the closed door back to the hallway. I could almost sense Sadie playing out in the family room. She seemed to be running in a circle and I started to get a little dizzy. How did I know that?

"And Sadie is…"

Rose sighed. "That little girl is the next Fae queen, provided she lives to the age of eighteen."

My eyes tracked along the wall as Sadie walked from the living room into the kitchen. "How do I suddenly know where she is?" I held up my hand, staring at it and remembering the splinter. "How did I know she was hurt earlier?"

Allura nodded. "The binding has already begun. Your blood is strong for a human. Your family comes from old stock, full of their own power. Let us complete the process so you may become the Guardian your brother wished for you to be."

The way she said that I could hear the emphasis on the capital G in the word. "Wait a minute. I can't be the guardian to the two little kids. I don't know anything about raising children."

"See," Rose said. "I told you he was unsuitable to the job."

The Counselor cleared his throat. "And yet, Princess, both your sister and his brother chose him."

"Wait, princess?"

Rose waved off the question. "We don't generally do titles anymore. Only those who serve the family still use them."

"But you're a princess? I suppose Lili was the previous queen?"

"No, there is only a Fae queen every five hundred years," Allura said. "Both Lili and Rose are princesses, as am I, though from another generation."

"Well, then maybe Rose should be this Guardian you're talking about."

"I wanted to be, but my sister overruled me. It has to be you, Chip. Let the Counselor explain all this to you and then you'll understand better."

I walked over to sit in the swiveling black leather chair in front of my brother's desk. I gestured to the Gnome to begin whatever it was he had to do while I wrapped my mind around what was happening. I didn't plan on accepting, but arguing the point was getting me nowhere. It was time to regroup and then try something different once they'd laid their cards on the table. This wasn't my first legal negotiation.

I could handle this. Right?

Rose

Chip sat in the chair as the Counselor flipped open the top of the brown leather satchel and pulled out a stack of file folders stuffed with papers. Then he surprised me and removed a laptop as well. I was used to most of his kind shunning new technologies, preferring to keep documents only on pen and paper, or parchment for the really important things.

Instead, the old Gnome set the laptop on the edge of Lili's desk on the other side of the room and attached the power cord to the back of the computer. He held up the plug, scanning the walls, looking for an outlet.

"Here," I offered, taking the plug from him. I leaned over the back side of the desk and plugged it into the power strip on the floor by the wall outlet. I stood up. "That should do it."

"Thank you, Princess Rose." He used two fingers to type something into the password spot on the screen and the screen opened to a still image of Lili and Bobby seated beside each other. Lili's pregnant belly and longer hair told me it must have been while she was carrying Sadie. She'd cut her hair short soon after her daughter's birth. That put the image at about five years old. It was probably soon after I'd been sent to test Chip for the role he now tried to weasel out of.

"Charles Henderson Proctor—" the Counselor said.

"Please, call me Chip. Charles Henderson Proctor is my dad."

The Counselor cleared his throat and began again. "Charles Henderson Proctor, Jr., you are named in the last will and testament as the future Guardian of the children of Princess Lili Eyely Eldersdottir and the human Robert James Proctor. This has been sealed with your blood, set into this document by my own hand." He held up a piece of yellowed parchment covered in beautiful, handwritten calligraphy. At the bottom beside the signatures was a dark reddish blotch.

"And that counts even if I didn't give the blood willingly?"

I rolled my eyes. "It counts, Chip. If you keep interrupting him, we'll be here all night."

"Sorry, Rose, I just have questions."

"Answer me this," I replied. "Would you give your blood to protect Sadie and Addison if it were necessary to do so?" I hoped for him to say, no, though I knew he wouldn't.

"Of course I would. I love those kids like they were my own."

As soon as he said it, I could see the change of perspective in his eyes. He knew that every word he'd just said was the truth, deep down, all the way to his soul. He may not have given his blood willingly at the time, but magic didn't care about such constraints. He'd gladly do so now, thus the spell sealing the document held. Perhaps it had even been strengthened through his realization.

Chip stiffened a little then arched his back as if stretching. "What just happened? A chill went through me. Did you cast another spell on me?"

I knew exactly what it was. It was something I thought I should be feeling. "It's the seal on the document. As soon as Lili and Bobby died, the magic activated. Have you noticed anything unusual lately, feelings or sensations you can't explain?"

He twisted his head to look over his shoulder, like he was staring through the wall into the rest of the house.

"You can sense her, can't you?" Allura asked.

Chip nodded. "When she hurt herself earlier, with the splinter, I felt it. Is that part of this, too?"

"Yes," Allura answered. "Other abilities may present themselves. The assignment of a Guardian affects the recipient in different ways."

"What kind of abilities?"

I hid a smile behind my hand at the look of concern on Chip's face. The hand to my face didn't fool Allura and she shot a stern glance in my direction before answering his question.

"I have no idea, Charles. They usually have to do with an individual's personality and other qualities yet to be discovered. You will have to watch and learn to master them so that you may protect the child until she is grown."

"But I know nothing about raising a kid. I have a business and a whole life in New York."

Here came the push back I knew was coming. Chip lived for Chip, first and foremost. As he caught up to what all this would mean for him, he was beginning to understand what it would take to be the Guardian to a future Fae queen.

"I suppose I could hire a nanny and move them to the city with me. I'll need a bigger place—"

"No." Allura's voice cut through the idle ramblings coming from Chip as he tried to make sense of all that had happened in the last few minutes.

"What do you mean 'no'?"

"I mean you may not shirk your duty by passing off your responsibilities to others. Your protective magic will help keep the princess safe, but only by reinforcing the power with your presence. Delegating the day-to-day tasks of care will dilute the energy. That shirking of duty could be disastrous."

"I'm very wealthy. I can hire the best security on the planet. No one will touch her." Chip's self-assured smile punctuated what he thought was an iron-clad argument.

I spoke up before Allura could, mostly because I couldn't stand to listen to him talk about himself anymore. "This isn't about you and what you could do in the past, Chip. Everything is different now. Accept that or step away permanently."

I saw the challenge of my words spark something inside him. He opened his mouth to speak but stopped himself and looked over his shoulder at the wall again, presumably at Sadie in the other room. A part of me envied that connection with her.

When he turned back to face us, his expression seemed more determined. "How sure are you that all this was an attack and not a horrible accident?"

Allura nodded at me to answer.

"I'll know more in a few days after my investigator reports back. However, Lili and Bobby were always very careful with everything they did once Sadie was born. They knew they had to stay hidden and not take unnecessary risks. The alternative was to expose their daughter to those seeking her location so they could take her eventual power for themselves. On top of that, the two of them possessed abilities of their own, including protections against harm from mundane things. Bobby was the Guardian before now. They would never have both died in a crash like that. The odds are stacked against it being accidental."

"Perhaps I have something that can help Mr. Proctor to make up his mind once and for all."

We all turned to the Counselor. He'd been silent during our discussion with Chip and we'd all but forgotten he was there.

The old Gnome tapped the keys on the laptop and the image on the desktop began to move. It hadn't been a still image at all. It was the first frame of a video he'd cued up to play. My heart leaped into my throat and fresh tears brimmed in my eyes as Lili spoke from beyond the grave with a message to the people in the room.

"Hello all. If you're watching this, then that which we feared the most has come to pass. Bobby and I had hoped to watch our little girl grow to adulthood, but that will not be. It falls to you in this room to ensure she becomes all that she can be, just as was done by those who raised me and Rose after Mother and Father died."

A twinge of long-buried anger rose at her words. Lili had been the first-born and thus was the focus of our parents growing up. I was nothing more than the backup child. In some ways, that gave me more freedom to seek my own path, but part of me always resented the attention she got over me. And yet we'd grown up close to each other, true sisters in every way. I squeezed my eyes shut for a second to try and stem the tears streaking my cheeks. Gods, I missed Lili so much right now. She'd know how to handle Chip over something like this.

I stopped my inner griping as Lili stopped talking and Bobby took over.

"Chip, you were the best big brother I could have ever had. You taught me so many things as I followed behind in your footsteps. You gave me the confidence in myself to become the husband and father I grew into. However, now I have to ask you for even more. If you're watching this, then I'm gone now and you've learned the truth about us, about all of Lili's family. My child is in great danger, and I can only turn to you and ask you to take up the task of raising her. Teach her what it means to be a Proctor. Rose and the others will make sure she learns about being Fae. You can make sure she doesn't lose her humanity along the way."

On the screen, Bobby reached into his shirt pocket. He pulled out a dark leather thong. Dangling from it was a wire-wrapped shark's tooth charm. It was the sort of thing you could have for a few dollars at any seaside resort souvenir shop.

"Remember when you gave this to me, Chip? I do. I wouldn't go in the water because I was afraid of sharks after you and I watched that old movie Jaws on TV. You found this shark's tooth and told me it was proof that the sharks couldn't win. You told me to believe in myself because a Proctor could do anything they set their mind to. That's how I know you can do this, bro. You may think you're not suited to the job or that someone else can be the Guardian to our child."

Bobby reached out and grasped Lili's hand, their fingers interlaced before looking back into the camera. "We both know that you're the right person to do this, to raise Sadie. We trust you to keep her safe and make sure Sadie grows up to become the queen she's destined to be. We know this because you taught me Proctors are capable of anything and you're a Proctor first and foremost. Thank you, Chip. Goodbye."

The video ended and the screen went blank. I wiped another tear from my cheek and sniffed back the start of a runny nose as I searched the room for a tissue. I caught Chip doing the same and we both arrived at the sole box of tissues held out by my aunt for us at the same time. He smiled through his bleary eyes and nodded for me to go first.

I took one and blew my nose, trying to gather my thoughts after hearing my sister's voice again.

The Counselor cleared his throat as he reached into his suit coat's inner pocket and pulled out a small brown envelope. "Your brother wanted you to have this, Charles. He said it would serve as a reminder of all you had to teach Sadie, and Addison, too."

Chip took the envelope and dumped out the contents into the palm of his hand. It was a gold chain. Dangling from the end was a golden shark's tooth, it's base wrapped in gold wire. It was almost as if they'd dipped the original shark's tooth in gold and added the necklace loop later.

The Counselor said, "Your brother had that made and Lili imbued it with magic of her own construction. It should be quite powerful in the right hands."

"Powerful how?" Chip asked.

The old Gnome shrugged. "That will be for you to discover. My guess is it will somehow work alongside your manifesting Guardian abilities."

For just a second, I thought Chip might turn it all down and walk away. Then he loosened his tie and undid the top button on his dress shirt. Releasing the clasp on the gold chain, he held it around his neck so the shark's tooth dangled just above the notch of his breast bone.

"Rose, would you mind helping?" Chip turned so his back was to me and he bent his knees so he wasn't so tall.

Realizing I couldn't say no at a time like this, I moved behind him and attached the two ends of the chain. I stepped back as he fixed it so it rested against his neck inside the collar. Two fingers of one hand came up and traced the outline of the shark's tooth as it lay against his tanned chest.

Chip started to say something but stopped and coughed to fix his cracking voice. "I, uh, I guess I can do this. They said I could rely on your help, though. Is that right?"

He looked to me and then Allura, waiting for a response.

"Of course you can, dear," Allura said. "We're all family now. Isn't that right, Rose?"

I resisted the urge to roll my eyes. "Yes, of course. If you ask for help, we will be there."

That seemed to satisfy his questions for now. He gestured to the folder full of papers on the desk beside the laptop. "Is there something I have to sign? I'm sure there are legal considerations in the human world that have to be attended to. I have already set up a separate trust for both children when each was born. I figured that was the least a rich uncle could do at the time. What about Bobby and Lili's estate?"

Allura let a rare smile cross her face. "Money is not an issue. As members of Fae royalty, the children will want for nothing, however, it is imperative that you and they keep a low profile. While we believe someone who wishes them harm is out there, there are many others who may not yet know where they are hidden. We must maintain them in this community until we know for sure."

"When will that be? Perhaps I should hire an investigator of my own."

I needed to stop that train of thought right away. "No, that will not be necessary. I have taken this matter in hand. As the family arms mistress, it is my duty to investigate this, and I will make sure to leave no stone unturned."

That seemed to satisfy him, and he turned to join the Counselor at the desk where the two of them flipped through the legal documents, human and Fae, until all the arrangements had been handled. I had to sign as a witness to Chip's signature a few times and then it was done. Chip Proctor was the new legal guardian in the human sense and the royal Guardian in the Fae sense. The children's protection now fell to his care.

"Charles," Allura said as Chip turned to leave the study.

"Yes?"

"While you are the final decision maker in all things regarding the children, it is our hope you will lean on us as often as you need regarding all things supernatural. Isn't that right, Rose?"

"Yes, of course. I've canceled all my travel plans for the foreseeable future. I'll be just a few minutes away at all times and will always be close to my phone. I think you still have that number, don't you?"

Chip tapped the slight bulge in his breast pocket. "It's right here.

I'll be sure to call as soon as anything unusual happens. Promise." He held up his right hand as taking an oath, though I was sure he meant it in jest. Knowing Chip, he was sure he could handle anything that cropped up with the children.

I smiled as he left the study. That self-assurance wouldn't last long if I knew anything at all about what might happen in the coming days and weeks. I didn't wish for trouble to befall Chip and the children, but since it was coming anyway, I'd relish swooping in to rescue him when needed.

6

Chip

As I left the study behind and returned to the thinning crowd of mourners still inside my brother's house, I realized how much of a shock it had been to hear Bobby's words in his own voice. I had never known that my simple gift to a little brother all those years ago had made such an impression on him. Mom and Dad had always told me he looked up to me. But in the way of little brothers throughout time, he'd mostly been a nosy pest, always trying to tag along with me and my friends.

I reached up under my tie and felt the outline of the gold shark's tooth through my shirt. They had said it possessed magic, something I would have discounted only an hour before. If it hadn't been for Rose removing the magical block that kept me from remembering how she had tested me for this duty, I would have remained happily oblivious to the existence of magic and werewolves, Fae, and whatever else the supernatural world held for me to learn.

I heard the giggling of small children in the family room and walked down the hallway to see what Sadie and the other children were up to. They'd settled down and were watching a cartoon with a family of dogs involved with some sort of garage sale or something.

Whatever was happening, the two neighbor children and Sadie found it all quite humorous.

When I came around the corner, though, Sadie's head snapped around, almost as if she'd sensed me coming. She jumped to her feet and ran over to give me a big hug around my knees.

"Wow, kiddo. What was that for?"

"I love you, Uncle Chip."

"I love you, too, Sadie. And guess what? I'm staying here with you for a little while to make sure you aren't alone. Won't that be nice?"

Mia's voice came from the stairs nearby. "Oh, so now you're staying. That changed fast."

She carried baby Addison in her arms as she descended. Strangely, she looked almost natural in the pose, as if she'd done this a hundred times before.

Mia caught me staring at her and laughed. "I'm the oldest of nine children, Chip. I've taken care of many young ones in the years before I became a model."

"I apologize. I guess today is a day full of surprises. Perhaps you'll stick around and help me get settled in here?" Having Mia around would be a lot better than asking Rose or one of the neighbor moms for help.

"No, sadly, I must go back to New York tonight. The agency called back. They can't reschedule the photographer for tomorrow's shoot. Don't worry. I'll call for a car and see if I can catch a flight back from Baltimore. You'll pay for it, yes?"

"Of course." I tried hard to hide my slight annoyance that while I was supposed to remain here, she was free to return to our jet-setting lives back in Manhattan. I heard a snort from behind and realized Rose had seen the whole byplay and probably read the signs of what had just happened as well as I did.

Allura and the Counselor walked past, headed for the front door. "Rose, be a dear and escort us out to my limousine. There's something we must discuss before I go."

While I wanted to know what they were going to talk about, sure it had something to do with me, I was pulled into the family room by

Sadie and introduced to the two moms from the other side of the cul-de-sac.

Barbara, an attractive blonde, and Ellie, a short, squat redhead, both told me how sorry they were about my brother and Lili. When I mentioned that I had been named guardian of the children, they each gave me their numbers and told me to call at any time if I needed help.

Barb jumped in first. "I have all sorts of time on my hands, ever since my ex-husband and I divorced. My kids are pretty self-sufficient, so if you need something, even in the middle of the night, you just call me."

Ellie slid in between us as Barb's eyes bored into my own in what was probably an attempt at a sultry stare. "Well, my husband Steve and I are around, too. Just call and one of us will come over to help out. Even though he owns an auto parts store, he's still pretty good with diapers and such when he needs to be."

Diapers, wow, I hadn't even thought about that. "Umm, I guess that's for Addison. Sadie's not still in…"

Ellie laughed. "Oh, goodness no. In fact, she potty trained faster than any kid I've ever seen. When she was two and a half, she announced she wanted big girl underwear and never looked back. I wish my little Stevie had been so quick to learn. But you know how boys are with such things."

Both Ellie and Barbara laughed at that statement, and I joined in, having no idea what was so funny about that.

"Speaking of diapers," Mia said. "This one is about due for a fresh one." She held Addison out at arm's length in my direction.

I caught a whiff of his rank diaper as soon as I took him from her. "What am I supposed to do with him?"

Mia looked at me and then at Barbara and Ellie and they all started laughing. Mia pointed back upstairs. "There's a changing table in his nursery. The diapers are in a basket right beside it. Make sure you use the strap and buckle him in. He's old enough to roll off at this age."

She gave me a gentle shove which brought on more laughter as I tried to put on an air of confidence while heading for the stairs.

Judging from their reactions, I had not been that successful at hiding my utter bewilderment.

Upstairs in Addison's room, I set him down on the pad atop the table beside his dresser. Mia had been correct. There were diapers in the wicker basket beside it, too. I unfolded one, examining it for a few seconds to get an understanding of how it worked. The tabs seemed to have a sort of hook and loop stickiness to them.

On the table, Addison cooed up at me with a delightful sound. I glanced down at him and melted as his bright smiling face beamed up at me. He had a definite look of his father about him, though I could see a bit of Lili in his eyes.

"Okay, Addy, let's do this." I made sure the strap was secured across his middle, took off my suit coat and rolled up my sleeves. I then returned to the scene of the crime and peeled back the tabs holding the front of the diaper closed.

I wrinkled my nose at the smell wafting up from the exposed interior of the diaper. "You'd think a child who was half-Fae would have poop that smelled of cinnamon and wildflowers."

Rose laughed from the doorway. "Poop is poop, no matter what kind of creature it comes from. That kid is a master of the stuff. He goes like three or four times a day."

"You're kidding," I said, hoping she was. I remembered what Ellie had said downstairs about boys. I couldn't imagine doing this four times a day every day for the next two or three years.

"I wish I was. I've been here watching Sadie and him ever since the accident. He's regular as clockwork. You'll see soon enough. At least he sleeps through the night. That's a bonus."

She handed me a plastic tub with moist baby wipes in it. I took a deep breath and dove in for the cleanup.

"I thought you had to talk with Allura and the Gnome guy outside. Anything I should know?"

Rose shook her head. "No, I sent them on their way. I'm supposed to meet my aunt back at her house once I'm sure you won't let the kids drown in their bath on the first night."

"Hey, I resent that." I said the words, even as my mind went through a new mental checklist about all the things I didn't know about taking care of kids.

"Don't worry, Chip. I love these kids as much as you do. I won't leave them in the hands of a rank incompetent until I'm reasonably sure he's at least partially prepared for the next twenty-four hours."

I smiled and nodded a thank you. "I appreciate that. This whole thing is a big surprise to me. I was sure you'd already been given the job."

"Nope. As you know from your recently restored memories, you've been first in line to take care of them for over four years."

"Why'd you have to use magic on me? I can keep a secret."

"Can you, Chip?" Rose scowled a little. "You were quick enough to share with your brother and the rest of the groomsmen at the wedding about our little hook up in the cloak room during the wedding reception. Wasn't that supposed to be a secret, too?"

"Look, I'm sorry about that. I was a drunk asshole back then. Things are different now." I took the dirty diaper, now piled high with soiled wipes, and looked around the room.

"Here, give it to me." She took the diaper, rolled it up into itself and secured it closed with the tabs. Then she dropped into a plastic waste container and stepped on a lever at the base. "That will roll each diaper into a little plastic sausage to contain the smell. When it's full, you just dump the whole long sausage of diapers in the trash and start over."

I slid the diaper under Addison's butt just as he let loose with a stream of pee all over my shirt and tie. Rose giggled and handed me a cloth rag from a folded pile nearby.

"Sorry, I should have warned you to keep that little firehose covered. He got me, too, the first time I changed him."

"If I didn't know better, I might think you left that information out just so I'd learn the hard way." I smiled as I said it. I figured the two of us needed to be allies, at least for now.

"I guess we'll never know. Here, use a fresh diaper. That one is wet now."

I took the new diaper from her and worked as fast as my inexperienced hands would let me to secure it in place. When I finished, I glanced at Rose. She pursed her lips and then nodded.

"Not too bad for your first time around. Before long, you'll be able to do that in your sleep. And believe me, you will."

"What?"

"Change a diaper when you're mostly asleep."

"I guess we'll see." I picked up Addison in one arm and grabbed my suit jacket with the other. "So, you're going to stick around tonight?" I didn't want to let on about my apprehension at being solely responsible for these two kids right away.

"Just until bedtime. Then I have to go and talk with my aunt. I'll have my phone with me, if anything bad happens. I've made sure the house has certain magical protections in place, but if you think there's an intruder, don't be a hero. Call me."

"You really think there's a risk to the kids? You haven't seen anything since you've been here, have you?"

"No, but that doesn't mean there aren't people with bad intentions out there. They'd be fools to challenge me directly, so that probably scared anyone off. But Sadie's very important and the ones in control of her growing up would stand very high in Fae circles after she becomes the queen. There are many who will want to wield that influence."

"I don't have any interest in that." I meant it. What did I need with such trappings. I had more money than I could spend in a lifetime right now. If I was careful with my investments, I never needed to work another day in my life.

"You may not," Rose said. "But there are others out there who've already killed to prove their determination. They will strike again." She fixed me with a level stare and then left the nursery.

I took what she said under advisement as we returned downstairs for the remainder of the afternoon. I was glad Rose was going to stick around. I had a lot of questions for her, once all the regular people left and we had the house to ourselves. There was a whole world I had to learn about as quickly as I could.

7

Rose

I led the way downstairs with Chip carrying Addy behind me. I admitted to myself he'd handled getting peed on for the first time reasonably well. Maybe he'd do better at this than I thought. That idea both annoyed me and pleased me at the same time. In the back of my mind, there was a little voice whispering to me that Chip might make a decent Guardian of the kids after all.

Sadie and the two neighbor kids were still watching the TV when Chip and I walked in with Addison. Mia, Barb and Ellie had just finished clearing the dishes from the dining room table and stacked them in the sink.

"Rose, honey," Barb asked. "Do you want me to load the dishwasher, too? It's no problem."

I held up a hand. "Don't ask me. I'm not in charge anymore. Chip's the one to talk to now."

Chip shook his head. "No, I'll take care of it. Thank you both very much for all the help today. I know the family appreciated it."

Ellie waved off the thank you. "No need to thank us. That's what neighbors do for each other. Come on, Barb. Let's grab the kids and I'll get you that casserole recipe on the way by my house."

Barb went into the family room and collected her four-year-old son Jonas and Ellie's daughter Meredith. She led them to the front door to meet Ellie who carried two recently cleaned casserole dishes.

"Ellie and I are just a phone call away, Chip. We put the leftovers in containers in the fridge and there are two other casseroles we didn't use in the freezer. Three hundred fifty degrees for about an hour until they're bubbling will do the trick."

Barb gave a wink as she followed Ellie out and pulled the door shut behind her.

Chip's smirk said he'd picked up on the implied invitation, even though he had a girlfriend.

As if on cue, Mia walked over to Chip and kissed him on the cheek. "My car is here, so I'm leaving, too. I'm sure you can handle this. I'll call when I get home and check on you."

"Don't worry, I've got enough here to keep me busy. And Rose is here for now."

"Only for a little while," I said. "After that, well, you make sure to call me if you need help?"

"Got it." He punctuated it with a thumbs up. Still holding Addy, he walked Mia to the door, gave her a one-armed hug and watched her stride down the front walk to meet the rideshare SUV pulled up out front.

When he returned, he asked, "So, I guess I should see about dinner for Sadie and Addison?"

I pointed to the kitchen door. "Addison has a few bottles made up in the fridge. He gets one before bedtime at around seven. The other is for breakfast. I'll show you where the formula is to make more, just follow the instructions on the canister. Sadie ate with the others already so she should be good for dinner."

At the mention of her name, Sadie looked back from where she sat on the floor watching the cartoon. She beamed a smile at me, and I waved back at her. That little girl was my whole world now, the only connection to Lili I had left other than Addy. If I didn't make any more mistakes, she would someday be my queen, too.

The thought of not being here tonight tore at me. Maybe I was being hasty, throwing him to the wolves like this. "Chip, I can stay and help you with bedtime or you can do it yourself. Sadie goes to bed just after you get Addison settled."

"I feel like keeping you here is taking advantage of you. I've got to figure this out sometime. Maybe a baptism of fire is just what I need. I've got your number. I promise I'll call if I need you."

Realizing this was my chance to break away, I smiled and walked in to give Sadie a kiss on the forehead. "You be good for Uncle Chip tonight, okay?"

Her eyes saddened and she looked around, realizing she was mostly alone for the first time today. "You're leaving?"

"Yes, honey. It's Uncle Chip's turn to stay with you tonight. You help him with Addy and then show him what a big girl you are going to bed."

She didn't seem quite convinced, but she gave a little smile and followed it with a meek little, "Yes, Aunt Rose."

I stood, knowing that if I didn't leave now, I'd find an excuse to stay all night. I didn't want to contemplate the complications that could bring up. Besides, Allura had been firm with her instructions about what I was to do next. I couldn't disobey her without good reason. She was probably right about leaving Chip to find his own way through this.

I waved to Chip holding Addy near the foot of the stairs. "Call if you need me."

He nodded and I left, pulling the door shut behind me a little too firmly. Maybe I was still angry at losing out and having to hand over responsibility to Chip. Instead of stewing about it, I channeled that anger into fuel to light the magical fires deep inside. I wouldn't be here to protect them directly, but that didn't mean I couldn't enable certain protections and alerts to let me know if there was trouble.

It was getting dark so I could let the deepening shadows around the home hide most of what I was doing. Spell casting required some movement with my hands and arms, though most of what I did required only verbal components. I made sure to keep away from the windows so Chip wouldn't spot me outside. He didn't need to know I was keeping an eye on him.

By the time I finished a half hour later, the sun had sunk all the way below the horizon and the welcome darkness folded around me. Instead of fear, I felt elation. I'd always enjoyed the night. It was quiet and usually meant I could avoid unnecessary conversation and interactions with people. It was also the time of the hunt and that was my primary focus. Somewhere out there was the person responsible for Lili's death. I had to find them and find out what they had planned next before they leveled an attack on Sadie.

That meant I had to face Aunt Allura again. The woman's sheer force of will had kept the family together through some dark times, especially after my own parents were killed. She made sure Lili and I grew up in relative safety. Of course, we'd both rebelled a little. Lili did it by going off to attend a human university and coming home with a human husband. I tended to rebel by running off to deal with supernatural problems around the world that required my particular martial talents. Now that I was home, I was sure Allura was going to remind me that I'd been absent when the attack happened. She wasn't wrong, but that didn't mean I needed her to tell me. I knew who'd dropped the ball on protecting Lili.

I walked over to my Firebird, still parked in the driveway, and climbed inside. The engine purred to life with a flip of the key and I drove off, hoping the wards I'd set would be enough to protect the two little ones I held most dear in my life.

It didn't take long to get to Allura's. She lived on an old estate just outside of town. This part of Maryland was firmly in the middle of horse country, and Allura's farm was known for turning out top thoroughbreds. I drove down the long, tree-lined lane, past long lines of white-washed fences and horses grazing in the fields. The home sat back where it couldn't be seen from the road. I turned down past the last barn and parked in the circular driveway outside the front door.

My aunt's butler, a longstanding Fae retainer named Reston, opened the door and showed me to the sitting room just off the main entry hall. I didn't have to wait long. Allura came in wearing a silk dressing gown. She had let down her long tresses of stark white hair, but I knew better than to think her relaxed. Her guard never came down all the way.

Allura glanced at the clock on the fireplace mantle nearby. "It took you long enough. I told you to leave him to figure it out on his own."

"He needed more help than we'd figured, and his girlfriend had to leave before I did. Are you sure this is the best course of action, Aunt Allura?"

"Did you enable the wards as instructed?"

"Yes, of course, but I could have done that without your direction. What we should be doing is watching the home. Whoever went after Lili is going to have to attack there sooner or later."

"Your talents, Rose, are best used out in the field. You've so often made that point to me in the past, I would have thought you'd agree with me."

"You're not telling me to leave for some other mission, are you?" I couldn't hide my shock at the thought. I wouldn't let her send me away.

"No, but you need to leave the care and Guardianship of the children to him. You must attend to the investigation. We must know who is behind this. I will expect regular updates from you regarding everything you find."

"Of course, but I already told you, I have the best investigator I know on this already."

"But, not the best woman. You should get out there, too. See what you can dig up among the Unusual community. There has to be someone out there who saw or heard something that would point to the culprit."

I'd been thinking much the same thing. However, I was perfectly happy to let Warren do the digging and see what he uncovered before I started following leads. Having me out there asking questions would only alert any guilty parties to lay low and avoid me.

"I assure you, Aunt Allura, Warren is a capable man, and he knows which rocks to overturn to find out what we need to know."

"I don't trust anyone other than family right now, Rose. You, of all people, should agree with me on that. Lili and her husband were betrayed, lured into going out at night on a fool's errand of some kind."

"How do you know why there went out? Did you talk with them that night?"

Allura's pained expression caught me by surprise. I'd never seen its like on her face before.

"Lili called me before they left. She said someone she knew had an important clue about your parents' untimely demise. I told her to leave it, that it was far in the past and not worth investigating. Instead of listening, she told me she'd be fine and that Bobby was tagging along as backup. The police called less than two hours later with the news of the accident."

"Why is this the first I'm hearing about the call? You should have told me. I need to look into her phone records and emails."

Allura nodded. "That is why you're not needed there at the home. Find out who contacted Lili and lured her out that night. They might not have been responsible, but they must know who is."

This new information changed a lot of things. Up until now, I'd had no idea why Lili and Bobby were out on that back country road so late at night. They'd left the children home alone and taken a great risk in doing so. Knowing that it might have shed light on what happened to our parents would have been one of the few things that would have clouded Lili's judgement. She'd long ago vowed to discover what happened to them. Either someone had real information, or they knew which buttons to push when it came to my sister.

"Very well, Aunt Allura. I'll follow this new lead and see where it takes me."

"Be sure to keep in close contact with me about everything you learn. I must know who this person was."

"Don't worry. I'll get to the bottom of this."

"Good. I won't spend any more time thinking about it." She walked back to the entry hall as the butler returned to stand by the front door.

I took the hint. My audience with my old-fashioned aunt was at an end. "Good night, Aunty."

"Good night, Rose. I'll expect to hear from you soon."

She walked up the grand staircase, ever one to make an exit, and disappeared upstairs. I smiled and shook my head. And people called me the drama queen of the family.

Reston cleared his throat behind me. I grinned up at him as I turned and walked back out to my car. I needed to call Warren and have him shift direction. Two sets of eyes on this new information would be better than just one. I'd track this down from the direction of Lili's phone and email records. He could start looking around for who would have knowledge of my parents and their final days.

8

Chip

"Come on Sadie, bedtime." I stood at the bottom of the stairs, holding Addy on one side while I beckoned to my niece to hurry it up. I tried to project calm and assurance, despite the anxiety I felt warring inside to take over.

Hold it together, Chip. You stare down billionaire dollar hedge fund managers for breakfast.

"I want Aunt Rose to come back and tuck me in." Sadie's lower lip pushed out in a pout as she trudged over to the foot of the stairs.

"I'm sorry, but it's Uncle Chip's turn to do that. Aunt Rose has some other things to do tonight."

"So, she'll be back later?"

"Um, no." My mind spun through choices to try and stave off the arguments of a four-year-old. I remembered my brother saying once that arguing with a toddler was a losing proposition. "But, if you get right to bed and fall asleep, maybe we can try calling her in the morning."

"So, you'll still be here in the morning?" She stared up with me, her bright sapphire-blue eyes wide.

So much of this little girl's life had turned upside down in the last week. She was desperate for some stability, something she could be sure of.

"I will be here in the morning and for many more mornings after that. Don't worry about that."

I tried to think of something else to say to reassure her, however my words so far seemed to have worked. Sadie started climbing the stairs towards the second floor. I followed her up, Addy shifted to the side in one arm, riding on my hip. This wasn't so hard. I could definitely do this.

I ran through what I figured the normal nighttime routine was in my mind. I'd helped put the kids to bed when visiting in the past and I tried to remember what Lili and Bobby had done.

"Okay, first let's brush those teeth."

I worked my way through the wash up before bed, including using a tiny baby-sized toothbrush on Addy on Sadie's insistence.

"He only has two teeth, Uncle Chip, but Mommy let him practice anyway."

That mostly involved him gumming the toothbrush while I moved it around a little inside his mouth. I kept it up for a few seconds and then rinsed the brush and put it back in the holder beside the sink.

Once the bathroom chores were done, I settled Sadie in her room looking at a book as she sat on her bed while I went in and put Addy down for the night. I plugged him up with the pacifier in his crib and laid him down on his back. He stared up at me as I reached over and turned out the light. The monitor was on the stand by the door with the camera aimed at the crib. The receiver was in the master bedroom. Bobby had showed off his baby surveillance system when he first got it set up.

I expected a bit of a struggle to get Addy to settle, and he fussed a little when I left the room and pulled the door shut, but he settled down by the time I got to Sadie's room.

"Okay, Sadie, let's get you in your PJs."

"I already did that, Uncle Chip. See?"

Her mismatched top and bottom left an interesting impression. The bottoms were on backwards and the top was inside out. However, she seemed so proud of herself, I couldn't bring myself to correct the issue. I figured it wasn't a big deal in the scheme of things.

I read her two books while we sat on her bed together and then I told her to lay down while I pulled up the covers. "I'll be right next door, if you need anything during the night, okay?"

She nodded; her lower lip started to stick out in that pout again.

"Now none of that." I leaned down and kissed her forehead. "Nothing is going to happen tonight. Not while I'm here."

"But, Uncle Chip, you didn't say good night to Bernard."

I was confused for a second then saw the stuffed dog she hugged tight as she lay there. I patted him on the head. "Goodnight, Bernard."

Sadie giggled. "That's not Bernard. That's Mr. Fluffles. Bernard lives under my bed. It's not polite to ignore him at bedtime."

"Oh," I said. She thought a monster lived under her bed. I smiled. "Alright, I will say goodnight to Bernard."

Getting down on my hands and knees, I lifted the ruffled skirt around the base of her bed, prepared to offer a sincere goodnight to the blank space beneath her bed.

Instead, I came face-to-face with a round furry face, with a pink nose, and protruding tusks that thrust up from the lower lip. The small, black eyes stared back at me, waiting for me to say something.

"Holy sh—!" I cut off my exclamation while scuttling across the floor like a crab until my back bumped up against the dresser by the door. The big round face stared out at me and for a second, I thought it was just an ugly stuffed animal toy.

Then it blinked.

Remembering the warning from Rose about attacks on the kids from supernatural forces, I pointed an outstretched finger at Sadie. "Sadie, honey, don't move. I'm going to come and get you after I deal with something."

A rumbling deep voice came from the broad face staring out at me from beneath the bed. "I didn't mean to scare you. I thought you were wishing me a good night."

"You can talk?"

Sadie giggled. "Of course he can talk, Uncle Chip. He's my bed troll." She said it as if it was the most normal thing of all at bedtime.

"Um, okay. It's nice to meet you, Bernard. How about you come out from under there so I can get a good look at you. You're kind of hidden by the bedskirt."

The figure beneath the bed grumbled something I couldn't make out and then crawled out from beneath the bed frame and stood up. He was only a little taller than Sadie's three and half feet. His head took up a full third of that size, followed by a relatively tiny body. He wore a blue zippered Adidas track suit top and bottom. Below that, his long, hairy, clawed toes poked out.

"There, you've seen me. Now can I get back to sleep?" Bernard asked. "It's been a long day with all the strangers in the house and I'd like to catch some shut-eye."

"What exactly do you do here? If you don't mind my asking."

"I protect the princess while she's asleep. I keep her bad dreams at bay, though that's been more difficult over the last few days with everything that's going on." He glanced at Sadie as he said it. "She's doing alright, though, aren't you, sweetie?"

"Yes, I am, Bernard."

"And you sleep under the bed? All the time?" I asked.

"That's my home. I manifest there after sundown, so where else would I sleep?"

He said it as if it were the most ordinary thing in the world. I guess I had a lot to learn about things in this house. It left me wondering something else, though.

I pointed out the door towards the master bedroom. "Is there a, a person like you underneath my…?" I trailed off, realizing I had a little trouble saying it.

"No," Bernard answered. "Adults grow up and don't need bed trolls to feed on their bad dreams anymore. When that time comes, we all move on to a new home."

"Uh-huh." I shook my head as I got back to my feet. "Okay, Chip, you learn something new every day."

Bernard took that as permission to climb back beneath the bed.

As he disappeared behind the ruffles, Sadie called out, "Goodnight, Bernard."

I moved back to the bed, careful to keep my toes away from the area under the edge of the bed. "Is that everything?"

"Yes. You'll be next door, right?"

"Right next door after I go downstairs and lock up the house for the night." I moved to the doorway and flicked off the light. The little rotating nightlight in the corner cast little moving shadows on the walls and ceiling. "See you in the morning, Sadie."

"Good night, Uncle Chip."

I pulled the door around but didn't close it all the way. I wanted to be able to hear anything happening in there and there was only one baby monitor. I'd already brought my overnight bag in from the car, and it was on the end of the king-sized bed in the master suite. I went downstairs and checked the front door and the door in the kitchen that went out back as well as the door into the garage.

With the house all locked up, I went back upstairs and sat down on the edge of the bed beside my bag. I stared at myself in the mirror sitting over the dresser against the wall.

I wasn't sure I recognized the person staring back at me. That guy had agreed to take over the care for two small children despite his complete lack of experience with the job.

"You stepped in it this time, Chip. You've got the biggest fund launch of your career coming up next month and you just took on another full-time job."

When my reflection didn't answer me back with a snarky comment, I shrugged and started to undress, changing into a pair of sweatpants and a T-shirt. As I pulled the shirt over my head, my phone buzzed on the bed.

I glanced at the screen. It was Eddie, my partner. Damn, I'd forgotten about calling him with everything I had going on tonight. I picked up the phone, swiping to answer.

"Hey, buddy, I was just going to call you."

"Are you on your way back? I hadn't heard from you and wondered if you still wanted to go over the new version of the prospectus the legal goons drew up for us."

"Um, there's been a complication. I'm still down in Maryland. It turns out my brother and sister-in-law left me in charge of the kids."

Eddie let out a barking laugh that went on for several seconds. "Jeez, Chip, you told them no thank you, right?"

My hand drifted up to touch the golden shark's tooth on the chain around my neck. "No, actually, I said yes."

"Dude, you know exactly nothing about kids. What are you thinking? We need you up here to kick off this launch. I've been lining up interviews on all the cable business shows for you next week. How are you going to do that if you're down there in Maryland?"

"We'll work it out," I said, wincing as I thought about all that I was leaving undone by staying down here with the kids. "Look, this is just a temporary thing until I get a few details sorted out. Once I figure out that stuff, I'll be back in the saddle, and we'll hit the ground running in plenty of time for the launch."

"If you say so, Chip. All I know is that when I was still married to Margo and had the kids at home every night instead of alternate weekends, it took up a lot more of my time than I wanted to admit. You've bitten off way more than you know."

"I said I'll deal with it, Eddie, and I will. You'll see. It'll be like nothing at all has changed. Email me the prospectus and I'll look it over tonight and send it back to you with any changes I think are needed."

"Suit yourself. I hope you're right, because the initial investors are going to be wary of jumping on board if you're not around to sweet-talk them."

He cut off the call and I laid my phone down on the bed next to me. I lay back on the bed to stare up at the ceiling wondering what I'd gotten myself into. I could do this, right? It would just take some juggling of things to keep everything moving forward. I started to think about how I could make the fund launch and childcare duties work out. It had been a long day, however and I soon drifted off to sleep.

I awakened to a long, loud wail from down the hall. It was followed by a thump and then the running of little feet down the hall and into my room.

I sat up just in time for Sadie to leap into my arms. Her moaning sobs wracked her little body as she clutched at me. I realized right away that she wasn't even really awake, so I just stroked her dark brown hair and hummed a song while I rocked back and forth.

A grunt from the door drew my eyes over to see Bernard standing there. He had his arms out to the side and he mouthed the words, "I'm sorry."

"What happened?" I whispered.

"A bad one snuck past me. I can't get all of them at stressful times like this. I think she saw a vision of their crash based on what little I picked up before she ran out of the room."

I wanted to scold the bed troll for not doing his job, but I realized it wasn't his fault. Plus, it was good to know what she was dreaming. Maybe I could help her talk through it in the morning, if she remembered it at all.

I nodded at Bernard, and he went back down the hall, leaving me rocking the future Fae queen in my arms until her sobs calmed down and her breathing became even and steady. Then I carried her back into her room and put her back to bed, making sure Mr. Fluffles found his way into her arms again.

I checked the clock as I returned to the master bedroom and realized there were only a few more hours until dawn. I dug in my bag and pulled out my laptop. Then I flipped it open and looked for the email Eddie had sent me the night before.

Opening up the prospectus, I started reading while I waited for morning to come. There was a lot to do in the coming days both here and up in New York.

9

Rose

I walked away from Aunt Allura's home taking some deep breaths as I worked to calm myself. That woman could be so infuriating sometimes. Her implacability once she'd made up her mind could be good, if she was on your side. In this case, she was not. Allura stood firmly in camp Chip, at least for the time being.

I pulled open the door to my Firebird and looked up at the manor one more time. I caught a glimpse of my aunt's face in the upstairs drawing room window. Even from here, I could make out her disapproving glare before she let the curtain fall back into place.

Fine, be that way, Aunty. There was more than one way to prove Chip was unsuitable as the Guardian of the next Fae queen. I intended to take every opportunity to prove I was the better choice, despite what my sister and her human husband thought.

I turned the key and waited for the engine to purr to life. First things first, though. I needed to beef up the wards in and around the home. What I'd left in place were adequate with someone like myself inside to bolster them and the defenses they activated. Chip had none of the training or magical ability to do it himself. That left me with seeking out more mundane and creative choices to protect the children when I wasn't there.

I dialed up someone I hadn't talked to in years. They might be the perfect choice to help me protect the home and those inside. While the phone rang, I pulled the car away from its spot in the long, curved driveway in front of my aunt's house. The phone picked up as I drove out onto the street and started back in towards town.

"This is Hitch. Who's this?"

"Hitch, it's me, Rose."

"You've got a lot of nerve calling me after all this time. I still remember how you left me hanging the last time I got mixed up in your machinations."

"I couldn't let that demon escape to wreak more havoc in the community. You know that. Besides, from what I heard, you landed on your feet."

"Only after a run in with the human police and courts. I couldn't make bail and spent three months in the local jail. You know what that's like for an Unusual like me? Huh, do ya?"

I rolled my eyes at the drama coming through the phone. Hitch hadn't changed a bit. "I'm sorry about that. However, it's not my fault they arrested you. I didn't know you were dealing drugs and had a full stash in your satchel when we went demon hunting together."

"I wasn't going to just leave my inventory in the car for someone to steal, Rose. I have to make a living just like anyone else. Selling spells doesn't pay the bills."

I saw my opening to break through the complaints and I took it. "Which is exactly what I'm calling you about. How'd you like to make some extra cash over the next few days?"

"It depends. Are the police going to get involved?"

I smiled. Greed always won out with Hitch. "Nope, not unless you plan on breaking the law. I need some special wards and defensive spells set up."

"What kind of spells? Who's it for?"

"I'll talk about that once we meet up. Where are you hanging out nowadays?"

"I'm down at Johannsen's by the tracks. I'll be here for a while if you want to stop by."

I didn't miss the chuckle at the mention of the bar downtown.

Hitch had to know the owner and I had a contentious relationship ever since I nearly burned down the place while taking down a fire elemental. Still, I needed Hitch's help, so Johannsen's it was.

"I can be there in about a half hour."

Hitch said, "I'll be here. See you then."

He cut the connection and I cursed to myself. There were too many places around town that knew me from my more rebellious youth growing up in the community. I picked quite a few fights with those who thought they could best a Fae warrior princess. I won every time, but not before the melee had trashed the establishment where the fight happened.

I took the time driving back into town to tick off the things I'd need from Hitch. He was a pretty good warlock in general, but he was a marvel at defensive wards and talismans. If anyone could come up with some creative ways to protect Chip and the kids without them knowing everything that was going on around them, it was Hitch.

That would be the trick. I wanted to protect Sadie and Addison first and foremost. However, I wanted to do it in a way that showed how Chip was out of his league and clueless to the danger around him. With the right things in place, I'd be able to show how my plans worked while Chip wasn't even aware of the risk to him and the kids.

I wondered how he'd done getting the kids settled earlier this evening. They were good sleepers, but kids would test boundaries whenever they saw an opening. I pictured Chip up and frazzled trying to get Sadie to stay in bed when she didn't want to. He'd probably err on the side of spoiling her when he needed to set the tone for what he wanted from the start. Give a four-year-old an inch and they'd take you for a mile-long ride.

I grinned thinking about him having a sleepless night as I pulled into the bar's parking lot. The building was right in the center of town, next to the railroad tracks that bisected the city's East and West ends. Johannsen's was in the heart of the downtown business district and judging from the number of cars in the lot, it was a busy night.

I took a deep breath and stepped out into the chilly night air. The cloudless sky overhead twinkled with a few visible stars competing with the streetlights at the center of town. Time to face Karl, the bar's owner. He'd thrown me out, but that had been almost ten years before. Surely, he'd forget the youthful sins of a twenty-one-year-old.

The double doors were propped open and I entered, turning right and going downstairs to the bar rather than into the restaurant on the main floor. It was closed at this time of the night anyway. The tarnished brass handrail on the stairs set the tone along with the dark wood paneling speaking of an old world feel dating back to the early days of speakeasies and rum runners.

Karl remembered those times well. During America's test of prohibition in the 1920s, Karl had made a fortune using his European contacts to smuggle in liquor through the nearby port of Baltimore. It was easy for him to do that as a vampire who'd originally been from Central Europe to begin with. I didn't know how old he was, but the number was closer to a thousand than a hundred. It wasn't polite to inquire about such things with his kind.

I reached the bottom of the stairs and walked up to the bar. I leaned against the wooden counter and searched the tall-backed booths in the darkened room for Hitch. I didn't see him at first. When I did find him, I wasn't surprised to see him standing with the vampire and pointing in my direction. Damn, he'd told Karl I was coming.

Well, nothing like ripping off the Band-Aid quickly. I had to take what was coming in order to get what I wanted. I pushed off the bar and walked across the room like I had nothing to worry about at all.

"Hello, Karl, it's been a long time."

Karl bared his fangs. "You've got a lot of nerve bringing yourself in here, no matter how long it's been. My kind have long memories."

"Oh, Karl, my family paid you for the damage a long time ago. Let's put the past in the past. There are a lot of things going on right now that need both of our attentions without you and me getting into a fight about it here and now."

He laughed. "You wouldn't last ten seconds in a fight with me, Rosie. I don't care what your pedigree is. The Fae have faded in power, and you aren't one of the warriors of old."

It pissed me off he wasn't letting this go. Despite his bluster, I was pretty sure I could take him if I had to. But that wouldn't get me what I wanted. I needed to come at this from another direction.

"What is it you really want, Karl? I can't believe you really want to fight me. The days of armed confrontation between our kind is long in the past."

"I suppose I could accept some token of apology for your past indiscretions."

There it was. He didn't want a fight either. He had something else he wanted.

"What did you have in mind? I won't kill someone for you."

"I can kill those who need it on my own, thank you," Karl said. "However, your aunt is standing in the way of me expanding my business to a second location in the southern end of the county."

It was my turn to laugh. "And you think I could change her mind about something like that. You know she bears old world grudges with the best of them."

"Yes, but I'd hoped in light of what I think you need from Hitch here, you'd convince her it's in all our best interests to keep the secret things secret. If she will stop her interference with the local liquor board's inquiry into my new location, then I will make sure to keep the things secret that I know." He shot a glance at Hitch who seemed very interested in what we were saying.

I got the gist of what he was threatening. He was one of the few in town who knew the true identity of our family and the connections to the old world Fae. He'd been one of the original settlers in this community when the clan had first come to America searching for a place to lie low after the succession wars that happened during the French Revolution. Certain factions used the human revolution against their nobility as an excuse to overthrow the Fae families who'd held power for nearly a millennium.

"That's a dangerous thing to even hint at, Karl." I lowered my eyebrows as I said it, letting some of my inner power light up my emerald irises. "I'm no recent college grad blowing off steam in a local bar. I've been out fighting the bad guys on the supernatural front lines for the last decade, and I've lived to tell about it. Don't turn this into a fight neither of us want."

"That's what I'm trying to point out, Rose. Our families have kept the peace for these long years without any problem. All I'm asking is for you to remind your aunt of that fact. Tell her my loyalty isn't in question as long as hers isn't either."

Well, that seemed reasonable. "I can do that, but you know how stubborn she is. I'm not responsible if she doesn't change her mind."

Karl nodded. "I have a few other irons in the fire besides this one. You do your part and I'll trust the rest to bring about the conclusion I want."

I didn't know what other machinations he had in play, nor did I want to. That kind of local politics was the reason I'd left town to go on my various quests over the years. I wanted nothing to do with local squabbles and feuds among the Unusual community.

"Then I'll call her first thing in the morning and make my pitch on your behalf. Does that mean I can have my chat with Hitch now?"

"It does. Don't forget to tip your waitress, even if you're not drinking."

"I'll have a few cocktails, and I'll be generous with the tip."

Karl smiled and dipped his head in farewell before heading back into his office down the long hallway.

I gestured to the dimly lit booth beside us. "How about here, Hitch. That work for you?" I didn't wait for an answer and slid into the seat.

He sat down opposite me. "How about you tell me what that mysterious conversation was all about? What's going on with your family and him that he can get you to back down like that?"

"I didn't back down, but I did trash this place all those years ago. I think he wasn't happy with the money my family paid to fix the place afterwards."

Hitch met my eyes and I could tell he didn't buy my explanation at all. He shrugged, though, and seemed to let the moment pass. That was fine with me. Most Unusuals weren't aware that we were connected to the Fae royal line at all, much less that we were *that* part of the family tree. Only the most loyal retainers were let in on the secret. For the others, we were just the typical, old-money Fae they learned about in the stories they heard growing up. That was why I had to handle getting Hitch to help me in a particular way. I had to make sure he didn't know what was up that required the protection.

"So, what did you come all the way in here to talk with me about? It wasn't to settle an old debt with Karl."

"No, it has to do with my sister's kids."

"Oh, yeah, I heard about that. I'm sorry for your loss. Lili was one of the good ones."

The way he said it inferred that I might not be, but I let the insult pass. "She was and thank you. There's a problem with some of the estate that goes to her children. There are some in our extended family who think they are entitled to it. They might want to make sure there are no heirs to inherit."

"Damn, you Fae are so touchy about things. Normal people just take things like that to court. You really think they'd hurt the kids?"

"It's a possibility. That's why I'd like to hire you to help me ward their home inside and out."

Hitch's face screwed up in a puzzled expression. "I can do that, Rose, but with you living there, who's going to mess with the kids? Your magic and other abilities are more than enough to do what is needed."

"I can't stay there. My sister and her husband named his brother to be the children's human guardian. Until I work some other things out, that's the way it has to stay. That means I need defensive spells that a total idiot can't screw up."

"You want them hidden from his view I suppose."

I nodded. "Let's just say the less he knows about the hidden world the better. He's learned about some of the odder aspects of the children's lives, but I'd like to keep him in the dark about what we're doing."

Hitch thought about the situation for a few seconds before he continued. "I'll need to get inside the home to work. If you don't want him to know what I'm doing, you'll have to get him out for at least a few hours."

"So, you'll do it? Perfect."

He held up a hand. "Hold on a sec. We haven't discussed payment."

"I know your standard rate for protection spells. Will it be more than that?"

"Hell yes. If you want to ward off Fae incursions, that'll take some extra juice on my part. Call it two-fifty an hour, plus expenses for spell components."

"Fine, but I'll want to see an itemized list of what components you bought and used. I'm not going to pay for you to stock up on things you need for other jobs."

I could tell from his reaction he'd been caught trying to cheat me. For a split second, I thought about grabbing his hair and slamming his face into the table. It would impress upon him the error of even considering cheating me in this job. I didn't, though. I decided it would only make me have to look elsewhere for the spells.

"We good, then?" I asked after he didn't say anything right away.

"Yeah, I guess so. When did you want to do this? I assume the sooner the better."

"Tomorrow or the next day. No later," I replied.

"It'll have to be the next day. I have to pick up a few things for the spells over in Baltimore. It'll take me most of the day."

I didn't want to wait the extra day. I thought my wards were good enough to warn me if I was close by to help out, but if I was going to investigate the deaths of my sister and her husband, I couldn't be tied to hanging close to the home. That was why I needed Hitch's help.

"Fine, two days. I'll call you to set up a place to meet in the morning day after tomorrow."

"That works. I'll need at least one hour up front to cover the cost of supplies."

I took a second to think about it before I dug into my large purse for my wallet. "I have two hundred. That'll have to do."

"I can make that work. See you in two days."

He slid out from the booth and walked over to the bar where he talked to the bartender for a second before handing over the cash. The bastard was using my money to pay off his tab.

I glowered at him to let him know I saw what he did.

He gave me a little wave and left the bar.

The waitress came by finally and asked me what I wanted. I

ordered a plate of wings and a beer. I hadn't eaten anything since the wake earlier and that had just been a few finger sandwiches. While I waited, I took the opportunity to start going down my list of suspects in Lili and Bobby's deaths. The sooner I narrowed down that list, the sooner I could make sure the kids were going to be safe long term. That was the most important thing of all.

10

Chip

I woke up as the sun poured in my window. I'd fallen back to sleep with my computer beside me. I sat up and couldn't figure out why my T-shirt was drenched in sweat. I kicked off the covers trying to identify the source of heat and found Sadie burrowed in against my side. The kid was like a giant hot water bottle with the amount of heat she generated. She must have come back into my room after I returned her to bed. For a little while, I just lay there watching her tiny face at peace in her sleep.

I tried to remember when she'd arrived. I was generally a good sleeper, but I'd like to think I'd have heard the little one come into the room and get up in bed with me. Still, here she was as proof that she could do it. I also marveled at the amount of heat such a tiny body put off and wondered if it was just her, or if it had some supernatural component to it. I made a mental note to ask Rose the next time she came by.

Moving with care so I didn't wake her, I slid out of bed, slipped on my sweatpants over my boxers, and tiptoed out into the hallway. Once there I did a quick check on Addy. He was still sound asleep in his bed. I checked my watch. It was just after six in the morning. Rose had mentioned they usually woke up around seven, so I figured I had enough time to sneak downstairs and make some coffee. I hoped there was some in the cabinets down in the kitchen. There'd been some served to the guests yesterday afternoon, so I was reasonably confident I'd be able to find it.

It felt weird to walk around Bobby's home like this without him there. He and I were both early risers and had shared more than one early morning coffee together around the island in their kitchen. Now I guessed I should call it my kitchen, or the kids' kitchen at least. This whole thing was still so new that I didn't know what was going to stay the same and what would need to change.

I opened a few cabinets, trying to remember where Bobby kept the coffee before I discovered the container along with paper filters for the coffee maker. I decided I needed a whole pot with what faced me ahead that day. In addition to watching the kids, I needed to check in with Eddie about the new prospectus. I'd taken the time before I fell back to sleep to look it over and there were only a few changes I wanted to make. Nothing too drastic, but Eddie would want legal to give it another pass anyway.

As the coffee started to drip, I pulled open the fridge and checked inside for something for breakfast. There was the left-over tray of cold cuts and cheese from yesterday in there, a half a dozen eggs, and a few other items that caught my eye. I decided on whipping up an omelet for myself. I'd spotted a box of pancake mix in the pantry next to the coffee grounds. I could make them for Sadie at least. I figured Addy would have one of the pre-made bottles in the fridge.

I cracked two eggs into a bowl and whipped them up with a fork while I added some milk and salt and pepper. I was just about to dump the mixture in the hot pan when a voice behind me caused me to jump.

"Ooo, omelets? That sounds delicious."

I spun around to see Bernard standing behind me. "Don't sneak up on a guy like that."

"Sorry, I heard you up and around and thought I'd come down for a bite to eat before going back up to the bedroom for some sleep."

"I thought you fed on dreams."

"I do gain energy from absorbing bad dreams, but who turns down an omelet? I need something to eat before hitting the sack. It was a long night."

"Lots of bad dreams?" I asked. I worried about what had gotten Sadie up and sent her into my room again.

Bernard nodded. "Yeah. I was able to handle most of them, but there was a doozie of a nightmare sometime around five that I couldn't get my arms around in time. It woke her and sent her scampering out to your room before I could do anything to help her."

"What was it about?"

The troll shrugged. "Beats me. I only get a general vibe from them. I knew it was going to be stronger than I could consume in one go. I think I lessened the intensity a little, but that was the best I could do."

I wanted to shout at him that it wasn't enough if she still had the nightmare, but I held my thoughts to myself. I still didn't know enough about how this all worked, and it looked like Bernard might be a resource for me if I stayed on his good side.

"I'm sure you did your best. She actually woke me up eventually. That girl can put out some heat. Is that a Fae thing?"

"Nope, but she does run hot at night. I remember her mother calling her a little heater from the time she was pregnant and then it continued after she was born. As far as I know, it's not magical in nature. Her parents never seemed concerned."

I smiled at the description of the little girl's ability as a spare radiator. It made me think back to all my previous interactions with the family to try and see if I'd missed any clues to the supernatural in and around their home. While I did that, I finished the first omelet and slid it off onto a plate which I placed on the island in front of Bernard.

"Pull up a stool."

"Don't mind if I do," he said and plopped himself on the barstool after he grabbed two knives and two forks from the drawer. He slid one pair over to me and kept the others for himself. He was far more dainty with his table manners than I would have assumed for a troll. But then, what did I know about them other than fairy tales and the odd movie?

I fixed myself an omelet and settled down to eat it across from Bernard. We had our breakfast in silence for a few minutes before the quiet was broken by a muffled wail from upstairs.

"Did you bring the monitor down?" Bernard asked.

"No, I forgot. I better go up and check on Addy."

"I'll come with you." Bernard scooped the remains of his eggs into his gaping mouth after which he smacked his lips around his upthrust tusks while he followed me out of the kitchen. "Good stuff. I'm going to like it around here if you keep making me breakfast."

"What did my brother do instead?"

"They'd just tell me to get myself some cereal and not to finish all the milk."

I reached the stairs and took them two at a time as the complaining wail became a more prolonged cry. I popped open the door to the nursery to find Addy sitting in his crib, crying. He saw me and held his arms up for me to pick him up.

Scooping him into my arms, I walked around the room trying to calm him by bobbing up and down and making shushing noises.

Bernard stood in the doorway shaking his head.

"What?"

"He probably needs a diaper and then a bottle. That's all he does right now."

"Right, diaper time," I said with a hint of disgust. I could do this.

I laid Addy down on the changing table and pulled out the wipes and one of the diapers from pile. He'd stopped crying and gurgled and cooed up at me while I went through the changing process. His one-piece pajamas were wet from his full diaper, so I changed him into a fresh onesie, struggling a little with the snaps. Then I added a T-shirt and little gray sweatpants like my own.

"See, kiddo, we match."

"I wanna match, too," Sadie said from the doorway. She rubbed at her eyes with her tiny fists to get the sleep from them.

"Okay, you're next." I picked up Addy and followed Sadie and Bernard into her room. The troll gave a quick wave and crawled under the bed to go wherever bed trolls went during the daytime.

Sadie had moved to her dresser and was struggling to pull out one of the drawers.

Shifting Addy to one hip, I said, "Here, let me help."

Together we searched her dresser until we found a pair of gray sweatpants with unicorns embroidered on the legs. I had to set Addy down which started him fussing while I helped her get dressed. She could do most of it herself but needed help with her socks.

Then the three of us went downstairs.

"I'm hungry, Uncle Chip. What's for breakfast?"

"Well, I wanted to make pancakes, but I have to feed Addison his bottle first. He woke up before you."

Sadie stomped a foot and balled up her fists straight-armed at her sides. "I'm hungry now. I should go first."

I might have been able to pull off keeping Addy's hunger at bay, but I'd made the mistake of grabbing the bottle from the fridge and he saw it. His whimpering grew louder until I plugged him with the nipple. He started chowing down while I tried to deal with Sadie.

"You can try to pitch a fit if you want, or you can help me get everything out so we can make pancakes together."

"Together? You mean I can help? Okay."

That worked like a charm. I walked around with Addy, feeding him his bottle while Sadie got out the things we needed. She had to slide one of the kitchen chairs from the table in the corner over to the pantry shelf to reach the pancake mix, but otherwise she was able to get most of the things we needed.

By the time she had gathered all the ingredients, Addy had finished his bottle and I put him in the highchair to watch while the two of us started work on the pancakes. It was fun to make them together and I think Sadie appreciated the opportunity to help out. We made extra-large pancakes and added chocolate chips. Once we were finished, we sat down to eat the fruits of out labor, along with butter and syrup.

"Did you used to help your mommy and daddy in the kitchen?"

"Yeah, I would help sometimes. Other times, they would tell me to go into the other room to watch TV or sit and read a book."

"Some things aren't foods kids can help with; you know?"

"Uh huh. That's what daddy used to say, too." She got a sad, faraway look on her face that sent pangs of sorrow into my chest.

"Let's talk about something else. What do you usually do after breakfast?"

"Don't you know?"

I shook my head. "I'm new to this whole routine, Sadie. That's why I'm asking you. Is there something you like to do? I could put on a video or something like that, or we could read a book for a little bit. I have to make a phone call later, but that won't take too long."

"Who's the call with?" She asked with a mouthful of pancake.

"A work friend of mine named Eddie. He and I have a big deal in the works, and we have to go over a few things. Do you think you can play quietly while I'm on my call? Once that's finished, we can go outside and play or maybe go for a walk."

"A walk? Like to the playground?"

"If you want."

She nodded so hard her brown curls bobbed around her face. She dug into the rest of her pancakes with gusto until she'd finished them.

I carried the plates to the sink and then picked up Addy and the three of us went into the family room, where I turned on the TV and set Addy on the floor in front of an activity toy I'd seen him batting at with his chubby little fingers yesterday. He sat up pretty well, but I propped two throw pillows behind him just in case he toppled over. Then I turned on the TV.

It took me a minute to figure out the way to turn the cable on to the right channel. I found a show that Sadie seemed to like from the guide and switched it on for her. Then I walked into the next room and pulled out my phone. Time to get with Eddie and figure out a few things.

Eddie picked up on the second ring. I knew he'd be up and at the office already. We were alike in that way.

"Chipster, I was hoping you'd call soon. Did you get a chance to go over the new prospectus last night?"

"I did. Check your email. I sent back the updated version with the changes I want."

"Changes? Dude, legal is going to have a hissy fit if you keep making changes. They say we're pushing the envelope with what the SEC will allow already."

"It's all in how you sell it, and we have to have everything locked down exactly the way I want it. Who's the most successful fund manager last five years running?"

"You are, but that's only because you play fast and loose with the rules."

"Eddie, what I do is make people money. As long as I do that, they don't care about the rest."

"Fine, when are you coming back up to New York? Those interviews I lined up are for in-person visits, not remotes from wherever you are."

"I'm working on that. I need to figure a few things out with the logistics of watching the kids. Once I get that done, I'll have plenty of time to get up there for the interviews prior to our launch."

"Just get a nanny like normal people do. You can afford the best after all."

"There are some family concerns to deal with first. I'll figure it out and I'll call you to lock in the dates and times."

"Okay, but don't take too long. I'm calling in a lot of favors to get you in with the Times and Journal."

"I know. Now let's go over the changes to the prospectus. You have it open in front of you?"

"Yeah, right here on my laptop."

"Good." I peeked into the family room to check on the kids. They were busy with the TV and the toys. "Let's get started while things are mostly quiet with the kids."

11

Rose

Hitch texted me two mornings later while I was in the drive-thru to get coffee.

I've got the things I need to set the wards. When r u picking me up?

I rolled my eyes. I don't know why he was in such a hurry. I figured I'd be waking him up even at nine thirty. He didn't strike me as an early riser.

I'm on my way now. Send me your address and be out front.

That should keep him. I didn't want him to think he was running this operation. The plan was simple. We'd drop in on Chip and the kids under the pretense of checking up on him. Then I'd distract Chip while Hitch went about setting the physical wards in and around the house. It shouldn't be too hard to keep him busy, I was sure he'd had a rough few nights with the kids on his own.

I paid for my iced coffee at the window and pulled away while I sipped at the energizing beverage. No matter what else I did in the morning, I looked forward to that first caffeine hit of the day.

Hitch waited as instructed on the corner outside his downtown apartment. He lived above an old music shop there. Most of the normal humans around had no idea its owner specialized in selling musical artifacts that had charms of various kinds. I'd had to stop in on several occasions and make sure he wasn't dealing in anything associated with the black arts.

I pulled in at the curb and Hitch climbed in the Firebird.

"Nice ride. Is it a replica or did you have it restored?"

"I restored it, mostly on my own. I added a few bells and whistles that weren't on the original sticker, but it's mostly stock."

"Can I drive it sometime?"

"NO!" I shot him a stern look before returning my eyes to the busy downtown streets. "Why would you even ask something like that?"

"I don't get much chance to have fun, Rose. I don't even have a car of my own."

I laughed. "All the more reason not to let you drive."

"At least show me one of the magical enhancements you added. What's it do? Can you make it fly?"

"This isn't Harry Potter, Hitch. We don't need people reporting a flying car to the authorities. I prefer to remain below the radar with such things. The less people know about our kind, the better."

Hitch humphed and sat back in his seat. I didn't care if he was disappointed or even hurt by my refusal. He'd get over it. I decided to go over what we were going to say when we arrived.

"When we get there, I'll do most of the talking. I'll tell them I was dropping by for a quick visit with the kids and you're one of my research colleagues along for the ride on our way to the university library at the edge of town."

"Right, don't talk. The way you command the conversation most of the time, that shouldn't be too hard."

"Look, Chip is smart. He'll pick up on something strange going on if you say too much. He's way too inquisitive."

Hitch thought for a second then asked, "What if he asks me a direct question about our work?"

"Tell him you could tell him, but then you'd have to shoot him."

Hitch's eyes grew wide with alarm. "You want me to threaten your brother-in-law?"

"He'll take the hint and shut up. Don't worry. I'll be there to back you up if he presses for any answers. Just don't say too much. He knows enough about my work to detect a lie if you let something wrong slip out."

"What makes you think he's not going to pick up on what we're doing? You said he was smart."

"Because, he's a single guy with no experience with kids. He's been alone with them for two days now. I figure he's reached the point where he's about to tear his hair out."

"If he's so bad, aren't you worried about the kids?"

"Not really. I figure the worst thing could be he's been feeding Sadie a bunch of junk food instead of making meals himself. Half the neighborhood brought over casseroles of one sort or another after the accident, but I'm sure he'll take the easy route and buy fast food for them."

I turned into the development where they lived, and Hitch let the questions drop. He opened his backpack and dug around in it like he was sorting some things.

"Everything okay with what you brought?"

"Yeah, I was reviewing how many items we have to place in and around the home. There's a lot in here. Are you sure I'll have time to get them where they belong?"

"I'll make sure you do. There's the house. Zip up and let's get ready."

I pulled in along the curb in front. Chip had moved his Tesla to the driveway. I assumed Lili's minivan was still parked in the garage. Getting out, I stood and waited for Hitch to extricate himself from the sports car. He wasn't used to a car that sat so low to the ground and he groaned when he stretched his legs beside the Firebird.

"What's wrong? You're not that old."

"Older than you are, my dear. Let's get this over with. I have places I want to go this afternoon."

I sipped at my coffee and took a deep breath. I was here to distract Chip and not to berate him for doing a bad job with taking care of the kids. I prepared myself for the worst and then opened the front door, letting myself in.

"Aunt Rose is here." I looked around the room as I called out for the kids and Chip.

"We're in the kitchen," Chip called back. "Come on in."

Hitch stepped in behind me. He clutched the backpack to his chest with both hands and scanned the open living room and the family room behind it at the back of the house.

"Put the backpack on over one shoulder like a normal dude. If you hold it like that, he'll be sure you're up to something."

"The energy in here is weird, dark almost."

"Of course it is. Two people who lived here just died and there's a lot of sorrow left over from something like that. Come on, they're in the kitchen."

I crossed the room, noticing the toys scattered around but not seeing any outward signs of the disarray I expected. I knew from experience Sadie alone could get all her toys out and spread around the room in a surprisingly short amount of time.

I pushed open the door to the kitchen and stopped as I took in the scene in front of me. Sadie stood on a chair pulled up against the island. She had flour in her hair and on her face and hands. Chip stood beside her with an apron around his waist. He leaned over, helping the little girl with the rolling pin as they pressed out some sort of dough along the floured countertop.

"Aunt Rose, Uncle Chip and I are making Chip cookies."

"Chocolate chip cookies," he corrected. "She didn't think I knew how."

"To be honest, Chip, I wouldn't have either." I felt a nudge from Hitch behind me and I moved all the way into the kitchen. "I dropped by to see how you're doing, but you seem to have everything in hand. Where's Addison?"

"Down for a morning nap. Sadie said he takes two a day. I kept him up the first day and paid the price for it. Hopefully today he's not as cranky the rest of the day."

I grinned, so it hadn't been all peachy after all. I was a little worried when I saw the house in good shape. "I'm sorry if you've had a rough time."

"No, you're not." He said it with a smile, but his tone had the conviction that he knew it was true. "What brings you by, besides checking on me. You could've done that with a call or text." He looked behind me at the doorway. "Who's your friend?"

"This is Hitch. He's one of my work colleagues who's in town to do some research at the University."

Hitch waved but didn't say anything.

"Well, make yourself at home. There's still some coffee in the pot over there if you want some. I see you brought your own, Rose, but feel free to freshen yours up if you want."

Seeing Chip in happy homemaker mode set my teeth to grinding and I had to force myself to stop. I shouldn't be upset that he was a good uncle to the kids. I didn't want him to hurt them, just fail at his job of protecting them so I could swoop in and rescue them.

"Don't let me stop you from your work. I want to stick around and try one of these cookies." I sat down on one of the barstools across from them as they resumed their work. I shot Hitch a stern look when no one was looking and jerked my head back at the rest of the house.

"Um, Chip, do you think I could use your bathroom? I just came into town and haven't had a chance to freshen up, if you know what I mean."

"Yeah, sure. The bathroom is down the hallway beside the stairs. You might have to move the potty stool out of the way. That's Sadie's because she's a big girl. Right, kiddo?"

Sadie nodded, a huge grin on her face.

As Hitch left to do his work around the house, I did my best to keep Chip distracted. "So, where did you learn to bake, Chip? I don't really see you as the kind who bakes cookies."

"Back in college, I got the nickname with the ladies as 'Chocolate Chip' because I always brought fresh-baked cookies instead of flowers on a first date."

"Really?" I said, genuinely surprised.

"Yep, it gave me an excuse to invite them over to my apartment for a night of baking for date number two." He gave me a wink at the end that left no doubt in my mind what the baking led to.

"Of course you did. Just when I think there's a tiny bit of redeeming nature to you, Chip, you do something to remind me exactly who you are."

"I've never pretended to be anyone else, Rosie."

There he was with that name again. I opted not to correct him. Better for him to think the nickname wasn't getting under my skin.

"So, Sadie, are you sleeping well with Uncle Chip here to take care of you?"

"I had a bad dream last night again. Bernard said he couldn't eat it like the others. But it goes away if I go in with Uncle Chip."

I looked up in alarm at Chip. "Bad dreams? You've met Bernard then?"

"Yeah, on the first night. Thanks for the heads up, by the way. It would've been nice to know there was a real monster under the bed."

I chuckled. "You weren't frightened of him were you?"

Sadie giggled. "He yelled and almost ran away, Aunt Rose. His face was funny."

"I'll bet it was." That made me feel better after him calling me Rosie. I looked back to Chip. "Did Bernard say anything else about the bad dreams?"

Chip shrugged. "Only that they were stronger than usual, and he couldn't get a handle on them himself."

"But you can, apparently," I added for him. "Any idea why you've got the magic touch?"

"Beats me. Maybe it's part of that Guardian magic you were talking about with your aunt and the Counselor."

I thought about what he said. He might be right in his assessment. I'd have to research that and see if that was a common power among the few human Guardians there were in the past.

"So, what's the next part of this cookie process?" I asked, changing the subject.

"Now that we've rolled out the dough, we use cookie cutters to make the shapes we want. We found a stash of them in the pantry. Most of them are for the holidays but there are a few that are more generic."

I watched as Chip and Sadie pressed out the cookies with the plastic cutters. They arranged them on two baking sheets. I looked over their handiwork and shook my head. "Where's the chocolate, Chip?"

"That's the secret. We put them on now, so they melt in blobs on top instead of melting inside the cookies like regular chocolate chip cookies."

He and Sadie started to press mini chocolate chips into the cookie shapes, eating a few of the chips as they went along. By the time they were finished, there were a fair number of chips on each cookie.

Chip took the trays and moved them to the oven racks before shutting the door and setting a timer on his watch. "Now we wait for the best part. Right, Sadie?"

She laughed. "The eating!"

"That's exactly right. The eating is the best part." Chip wiped his hands on a dish towel and started gathering up the kitchen tools and cleaning up the island countertop. "Hey, where's that friend of yours? He's been gone a while."

"You keep cleaning up. I'll go and check to make sure he didn't fall in or something."

"Just as long as he's not robbing us blind."

I excused myself and left the kitchen, bumping into Hitch as he was returning from his mission. "Here he is. I was just coming to search for you."

"Sorry," Hitch said. "I'm afraid travel disagrees with me." He patted his stomach and frowned.

"Can I get you an antacid or something?" Chip asked.

"No, no, I'll be fine, but perhaps, Rose, you and I could make our way on up to the University. They have a room for me there. I think taking a little time to rest will do wonders for me."

"Uh-oh, I suppose we'll have to leave without any cookies. You'll have to make them for me again when I come back, Sadie."

Chip smiled. "We never did have a second date, Rosie."

"We never had a real first date, Chip. Remember that?" I looked at Sadie. "Give your brother a hug when he wakes up from his nap for me."

"I will." She ran around the island and gave me a big hug around my waist, leaving flour-white hand and face prints on my black jeans. I rolled my eyes. Perfect.

I hugged her back and then left with Hitch. As soon as we got outside, I asked, "Did you make sure to cover the whole house?"

"Everything but the kitchen. There was no way in there with everyone around. I placed some extra items in the family room beside it though. That should help if anyone comes in the back door."

"It'll have to do. Come on. I'll take you back downtown."

"And pay me."

"Yes, and pay you. Remember that money also pays for your silence on this matter. If I find out you've been talking about this, I'll hunt you down myself and no one will ever find you."

Hitch gulped.

I smiled and pointed to the Firebird. I liked to leave an impression with the people I worked with, especially those like Hitch who lived in the gray areas between the light and the dark. I was not one to be trifled with.

Chip

That night, I woke to a sound I'd never heard before. It simultaneously terrified me and sent chills down my spine like fingernails scratching on an old-school blackboard. If I had to describe it for someone, I'd probably come up with a cross between an angry dog's howl and the screech of tires trying to stop before a horrible accident.

It sat me upright in bed and my first thought was to check on the kids. I passed by Addy's room first. He was sound asleep, but there was a white noise machine in there that played at night. It probably covered up some of the noise, whatever it was.

I stopped outside his door as I closed it, listening. I heard more sounds of movement coming from downstairs. I peered down the upstairs hallway towards the steps but didn't see anything in the dark.

The creak of a door behind me alerted me that Sadie had heard the sound, too. I looked back at her room. Sadie's little head popped into view with Bernard's right above it.

"Uncle Chip?"

"Go back into your room, Sadie," I whispered. I thought about what else to tell her. "Get under the bed with Bernard. We're going to play hide and seek for a little bit. You be extra quiet, okay?"

She nodded, but the frightened look didn't leave her face as she disappeared back into her room. Bernard had emerged from beneath the bed in the background. He gave me a quick thumbs up before coming over and closing the door.

Okay, the kids were safe. Now it was time to see what made that God-awful noise. I snuck along the dark hallway and looked downstairs. It was so dark I couldn't see anything beyond the first few steps lit by the upstairs hallway nightlight. I went down a few steps as I tried to pierce the darkness.

A stone-cold sensation pressed against my chest, and it took me a second to realize it was Bobby's shark's tooth pendant on its chain around my neck. I absently reached up to move it around. As I touched it through my T-shirt, there was a flash of light and the darkness faded to a twilight of grays and muted color vision that allowed me to see much better.

I didn't even question how that had happened. I didn't have time. I continued down the steps, able to see now where I couldn't before. I reached the landing and turned the corner, looking out over the railing. Something large writhed on the floor in front of the sofa. Soft grunting sounds come from it as it moved. Had some animal broken through the back of the house somehow and gotten injured inside?

Walking down the rest of the steps, I moved to the back of the sofa to see if it was a deer or maybe a large dog. I leaned over and came face to face with what I could only describe as a cross between a large hairy man and a big cat like a lion. The stripes on its furry arms told me it was not a lion, but a tiger, as crazy as that sounded.

The beast snarled and swiped at me with a clawed hand.

I jumped backward to escape its reach.

It pulled its arm back right away with a groan to clutch at something in its chest. I looked closer and realized the brass fireplace poker had somehow become imbedded in its heaving torso.

Horrified, I backed away, only to whip around at a sound behind me. There was another of the cat-beasts standing on two legs behind me. It wore ripped jeans and a similar black T-shirt as its companion.

I froze for a split-second.

That was long enough for it to attack. It leaped forward at me.

I flung out a hand in defense to ward off the creature.

It stopped suddenly in mid-air as if it slammed into a glass wall. The cat-beast landed on its feet and pushed at the invisible barrier, trying to get at me. I could feel its strength pushing against my outstretched hand. It threatened to heave me over with the force of its blunted charge.

I stepped backward, angling towards the stairs. I moved carefully, knowing a misstep would result in me getting knocked over by the powerful push of the creature I somehow held at bay.

While my barrier was strong enough to withstand the attacks, the force of those attacks still reached my outstretched arm, threatening to buckle the only defense I had. I needed to get past it and up the stairs to put myself between the beast and the kids.

I decided to make a break for the landing while the tiger-man rebounded from another charge at the invisible barrier.

When I turned towards the stairs, the barrier came down and the creature bounded across the room in my direction. A rattle from the bookshelf to my right warned me of something coming from that direction. I barely had time to duck as every single hardcover book from the shelf flew outward in my direction.

They passed over my crouched form and slammed into the big cat-man in mid-leap. It collapsed to the ground, but immediately rose and tried to reach me. The books kept hitting it, though. The force of each impact pushed it back a half step. It snarled in anger at being defied in its goal to reach me.

Realizing I had the break I needed, I raced up the stairs. I stopped halfway down the hallway to grab Addy from his crib and then I ran for Sadie's room.

I darted inside and slammed the door behind me. Addy started to cry in my arms as I turned the little bedroom door lock in the center of the knob.

"That's not going to stop a weretiger, Chip," Bernard said from beneath the bed.

"W-w-weretiger? Was that what they were?"

"I smelled them when Sadie opened the door. How come they didn't kill you?"

I shook my head. "No idea. Right now, the bookshelf is holding them off. Come here and help me barricade the door. Sadie, go and sit in that chair in the corner. I'm going to give you Addy to hold. Don't let go of him."

She did as I asked, and I placed the screaming baby in her arms. Her frightened eyes gazed up at me. "Is it going to be okay, Uncle Chip?"

"It will be fine. I won't let anything happen to either of you." As soon as I said it, I felt a calm assurance that what I said was the truth. The shark's tooth chilled against my chest again at the same time a roaring snarl sounded from down the hallway outside.

Bernard had already slid Sadie's dresser in front of the door. I joined him to press my shoulder up against the chest of drawers and try to hold the door closed.

The door shuddered as the weretiger slammed into it. The blow popped the door open, breaking the pitiful lock and splintering the door jamb in the process. The tall dresser rocked back against Bernard and I, but we shoved it back upright and pressed the door closed again.

More blows rocked the door accompanied by more angry roars from the other side. Each time Bernard and I managed to press the attack backward.

"How many were there?" the Troll asked.

"Two. One was incapacitated by someone or maybe something else. Does the house have defensive magic of its own?"

"Not that I know of. Maybe Rose could tell you. I'm just in charge of the kid's bedroom and dreams."

Slam, slam, slam.

More blows rocked the chest as the door began to come apart on the other side. I knew I had to try something else. I reached for my pocket and realized I didn't have my phone. It was still on the night-stand by my bed, so I couldn't call Rose, or the police, or whoever you called when monsters attacked your home.

The cold of the shark's tooth drew my attention again between attacks on the door. I'd somehow stopped it before. Maybe I could do that again. I could still see in the dark so maybe the other power was still there, too.

I waited for another hit on the door and pressed it back with my shoulder against the dresser. Then I stood upright and held out my hand as I'd done downstairs. The top of the door had been shredded by tiger claws. I could easily see the weretiger on the far side of the partially destroyed door.

I threw my hand forward, palm out. "Stop!" My shout filled with all my will, and I mentally pressed at the beast with the outstretched hand.

To my amazement, the weretiger slid back a few feet on the carpet.

Judging from the startled expression on the partially human face, he was surprised by the force of my attack, too. Of course, it only seemed to be a barrier and not really an offensive weapon. It would be much better if I could wield an invisible sword or something like that while keeping the beast at bay.

Once more, I felt the force of its powerful, muscular body trying to push past the hidden barrier I'd placed in its path. I braced my feet and leaned over the top of the dresser while I pushed back as hard as I could. I had stopped it for now.

The weretiger wouldn't give up, though. It charged at us again and again until its breathing came in ragged gasps.

I knew exactly how it felt. My outstretched arm ached from the force of its attacks slamming into it and my mind grew foggy. Trying to think about what to do next felt like wading through jello. Everything was happening in a haze, and it was harder and harder to concentrate.

Behind me I heard Sadie singing softly to Addy. He'd stopped crying for the most part, though an occasional whimper escaped him. I didn't dare spare a look back at the two of them, but I could sense in my heart they were okay for now, just a little scared.

After pounding at the barrier for almost fifteen minutes, the weretiger stopped and stood at the end of the hallway glaring at me. His feral feline eyes glowed yellow in the twilight of my enhanced vision. "We'll be back," he growled. "You can't stop us forever. We will have the girl."

"Not if I have anything to say about it." My bravado sound good, despite the weariness I felt all the way to my bones from withstanding the beast's attack. If there had been two of them able to bring the fight, I'm not sure I would have been able to hold them off.

The tiger man huffed one last time at me then raced back down the stairs at the far end of the hallway. I heard a low keening wail from downstairs and some more movement, then there was nothing.

I didn't dare let down my barrier. It could be a trick of some sort and I didn't know if I'd have the strength to bring it up again if they returned. So, I stood there with my arm aimed down the hallway, holding the invisible wall in place against anyone who would harm the two kids. I figured I just had to hold out until sunrise, or until some sort of help arrived.

13

Rose

Warren waved at me as he strode into the all-night diner. He slid into the booth across from me. The waitress arrived to at the same moment to see if he wanted anything.

"Coffee, black," he said.

She nodded. "I'll be right back. Can I freshen your coffee, too, hon?" She directed the last at me.

"That'd be great."

I waited until she stepped away before I leaned across the table in Warren's direction. "What's so important that you had to meet up tonight. We could've gotten together tomorrow like we'd planned."

"I got that contact at the coroner's office to forward me the autopsy reports on what little they found of your sister and her husband in the burnt wreckage."

"What did they say that we didn't already know?"

"There's evidence they were already dead when the fire was started. I don't understand all the medical mumbo jumbo, but to me it's proof there was foul play. The human authorities are still saying it was an accident, but this tells me otherwise."

"That couldn't have waited until tomorrow?" I rubbed at my right temple, trying to stave off the migraine I was getting from lack of sleep.

"There was more. They did DNA testing on the remains to confirm it was Lili and Bobby. There was a third set of DNA found at the scene labeled as feline."

That puzzled me. "They don't have a cat, and if they did, they wouldn't have taken it with them in the SUV that night."

"The feline DNA was sent off to the Maryland Zoo for animal typing in Baltimore. They said it was from a tiger."

That caught my attention. There was only one way a tiger was loose in the middle of this investigation. "As in weretiger?"

"That's what I'm thinking." Warren's frown said it all about what he thought of the feline were-creatures. "I checked with a few pack members I trusted to keep it quiet. They said there aren't any of them in the Unusual community around here. I thought you'd want to know in any case. The big cats don't come out to play without some powerful backing behind them."

I tried to think about the implications. Warren's findings confirmed my suspicions that it wasn't an accident. That also meant that the kids were definitely in danger, too. Someone either wanted to take them or kill them. Neither option was acceptable, of course. Weretigers were notorious for their viciousness and only went to work for the highest of bidders. Someone with substantial resources had come after Lili and her family.

I leaned back as the waitress returned with the coffee for Warren and tipped the pot over my cup to freshen up my remaining half cup.

I lifted the cup to take a sip. "Thank you."

"You're welcome. Now, are you sure you don't want some pie? There're two pieces of lemon creme left if you want them."

"No, that's alright. We won't be here much longer," I replied.

"Okay." She fished in her apron and pulled out the ticket with the two coffees on it. "Here's your bill. You can pay me or at the register up front."

"Thank you." I fished into my purse and slid a twenty-dollar bill under the ticket.

Warren raised his eyebrows. "Big spender for two coffees."

"We're her only customers. She's living off of tips alone on this shift."

He smiled and leaned back to drink his coffee. "Hey, you do you. I'm just saying you never tip me like that."

"I pay you very well for your services, Warren. If you want a tip, you come here and wait tables for a living and I'll leave you one." I sipped at my coffee. "Anything else in the report."

"Nope, but I figured this was important enough to tell you right away. Those tiger folk don't mess around. And they mostly work alone or in small family groups. Their kind isn't like my pack. If we had one, a local weretiger family would notice if someone new was in town."

"I'll keep that in mind. What did the human coroner's report say about the tiger DNA?"

Warren laughed. "What they always do when they encounter something that gives a glimpse of the Unusual world, they write it off as an anomaly with a contaminated sample, or some such nonsense."

"I'm always amazed that more of the human leadership doesn't know about our hidden world. There's plenty of evidence to clue in the population out there. I mean, there was that zombie outbreak in Elk City last year. They explained it away as a random virus outbreak."

"I guess people just want to live their lives, Rose. They don't want to live through the excitement of adventures the way you do."

I shook my head. "I guess so. It's alien to me to think that way—Ow!" I stopped as a stabbing pain hit my right wrist. It took me a second to realize it was the charm bracelet chain Hitch had given me. It was linked to the wards in the house. "Oh, no. Something has tripped the interior wards at Lili's house. Whoever it is has already gotten inside. I have to go."

I slid out of the booth and raced for the door. Warren ran right behind me. He didn't say a word as he climbed into the passenger seat of the Firebird. I didn't tell him to leave. I might need the backup.

I gunned the engine and peeled out of the parking lot as I drove to get to the kids as fast as I could.

Warren fumbled with the seat belt as I whipped around a corner at the edge of town. Then he steadied himself with a hand clutching the arm rest and the other splayed against the dashboard.

I didn't care if he was uncomfortable with my driving. I focused on getting to the house. I pounded on the top of the steering wheel with a fist. I was too far away. It would take me at least ten minutes to get there. I prayed the countermeasures Hitch had installed with his spells would stop whatever attack was happening.

Even at the breakneck speed I was driving, it felt far too slow as the minutes ticked by and the pain from the bracelet continued to throb against my wrist. I almost lost control of the powerful sports car when the turn for their development came up. I spun the wheel and the back end of the Firebird whipped around, almost completing a full three hundred sixty-degree turn.

I regained control by braking to slow a little, then jammed my foot back on the gas to drive straight into the development's main road. It was the middle of the night, so I wasn't worried about kids playing near the street, thank the gods.

When I screeched to a stop in front of the house, I popped the door, leaving it open as I ran for the front door. It stood ajar. I wondered why the spells I had placed outside days before hadn't alerted me to the trouble sooner, but I shoved the thought away. There'd be time to figure that out later.

I burst inside and looked around. The living room and family room looked like a tornado had hit it. I smelled the coppery tang of blood in the air, causing my worst fears to rise up in my mind. Had I failed to protect my family again?

"Sadie! Chip! Where are you!"

I knew I was screaming, but I didn't care. Fear and anger drove me at this point.

I heard Chip's voice first. "Up here, Rose. We're all in Sadie's room."

Warren was just coming in the door behind me as I ran to the stairs, taking them three at a time, leaping from step to step until I reached the top. I didn't remember grabbing my silver sword from its scabbard behind my driver's seat, but I had it in my hand now. It gleamed in the dimness of the upstairs hallway, the magic in the blade giving off a little light.

I saw the shredded remains of the bedroom door at the end of the hallway. There was something pushed up against the door from the inside, though I didn't know how Chip had managed to hold off whatever had done that type of damage.

"Chip, are you there?"

"In here," he called out. "We're okay. Are they gone? We haven't heard anything downstairs for a while until you came in."

I moved to the door and looked inside Sadie's room through the broad holes ripped in the top of the door. They'd pushed the bureau against the door to barricade it. Chip had collapsed back to sit on the bed. He looked positively ragged.

"Move this, I want to come in."

Chip struggled to his feet. He and Bernard came over and slid the dresser to the side. As soon as it moved out of the way, the remains of the door collapsed into the room in splinters.

I stepped over the debris, searching for Sadie. She sat in her comfy reading chair in the far corner, holding Addy in her tiny arms. The baby had fallen asleep.

"Oh, thank the gods. You're all okay."

"What the hell were those things that attacked us? Bernard called them weretigers. Is that a thing?"

I nodded. "They are very much a thing." I looked back at Warren, who was coming down the hall now. "Did you hear that?"

"I did. I can smell them, too. How many were there? I can tell it was more than one."

Chip said, "There were two that I saw. One got injured downstairs. The fireplace poker had impaled him somehow. He must've tripped over it or something. I think it was his cry of pain that woke me. I saw him lying by the sofa when I went down to see what made the noise."

"You went down to face them?" I said. "Are you insane? You're lucky to be alive."

"Hey, calm down. I saved the kids, didn't I?"

"Don't tell me to calm down, Chip. If there's danger, your first duty is to ensure the kids are safe."

"How was I supposed to know it was weretigers? I didn't even know that was a thing until tonight. I thought an animal had gotten in somehow and injured itself."

Warren snorted a chuckle. "You weren't wrong."

I stabbed at the werewolf with my eyes.

He closed his mouth and left to go back downstairs. He'd check around and make sure the attackers had really left.

"Look, Chip, I'm glad you're all safe. The attack had me worried, that's all."

Chip's head tilted a little to one side in thought. "About that, how did you know there was an attack? I didn't call you. My phone's still in my room."

"I had wards set inside by Hitch the other day. I'm glad I did. The basic wards I placed outside didn't alert me. They must've detected them and disabled the spells to get inside."

"Wait a minute. You put spells inside to protect us and you didn't tell me?"

I gave Chip a level stare. That usually made people look away when I didn't want to answer them.

Chip didn't flinch.

"Fine, I should've told you. It looks like it worked, though. You said the fireplace poker stabbed at one of them. Judging from the whirlwind that hit downstairs, other defenses went off as well."

"The bookshelf attacked the second one, but that only slowed him down. I did something on my own to stop him once he got upstairs. I don't know what, but somehow, I was able to hold him back."

That surprised me. "What do you mean? You were able to attack them with magic?"

"I mean just what I said. It wasn't an attack. It was more like a clear shield that kept the weretiger back. I guess it was magic, though. I didn't really think of it that way until now. I just did it because something had to stop it from reaching us."

I looked him up and down, then looked over at Sadie. Bernard had disappeared back under the bed. "You all look good, considering."

"We're fine, though I feel like I need to sleep for several days. It's an exhaustion like I've never felt before."

"That's the mana drain."

"The what?" He asked.

"Mana is your store of magical energy. There's some mana in all living things, even those that don't use magic. When you became the Guardian, I told you some abilities might manifest themselves. This shield you put up must be one of them."

"How does the mana figure in?"

"The more you use your abilities, the larger the drain. You only have a finite amount, though you can increase it over time through practice."

"I wish someone had explained this to me before tonight. It would've been helpful to know some of the details of how magic works."

I shook my head. "I didn't think you'd need to know. I thought my wards and what Hitch put in place would be enough."

"Well, they weren't. From now on, Rose, you need to level with me. We can't have any secrets where the kids are concerned." Chip glanced over at Sadie and Addy in the chair. "Let's get them back to bed, then we can finish this conversation downstairs while we clean up."

I caught Sadie's big eyes gazing at the two of us arguing in her room and realized he was right. I propped my sword by the door and walked over to her.

"Give me Addy, sweetie. I'm going to put him to bed."

She lifted him up so I could scoop him up in my arms. He squirmed a little against my embrace but didn't awaken.

"I'll meet you downstairs after you get her settled."

Chip nodded and I left with Addison. This discussion wasn't over. There was a lot we had to work out tonight. Things were a lot more dangerous than I'd thought.

14

Chip

Rose left with the baby, and I looked at Sadie in the chair. Her lip pushed out in a pout and tears welled up in her eyes. I crossed the room to her and scooped her into my arms.

"It's going to be alright. I promise."

Her little arms squeezed tight around my neck as I walked back and sat on the edge of her bed. I held her a little longer until her grip relaxed a little. Then I twisted and settled her down in bed.

"I'm scared, Uncle Chip."

"That was scary for me, too, but I'll never let the baddies get to you. Bernard's here too, right Bernard?"

A grunt from the troll under the bed indicated the affirmative answer.

I pulled up the covers and tucked them in around her. "Aunt Rose and I are going to be downstairs. If you need us, you call and we'll come right up."

She opened her mouth wide in a yawn and I took the cue and stood up. "I'll come up and check on you in a little bit. Close your eyes, sweetie, and go to sleep. Uncle Chip's here for you."

She did as I asked, and I stood watching her until her breathing became even and I was sure she was asleep. I picked my way through the wreckage of the door in my bare feet, careful not to make any noise. Then I went downstairs.

Rose and her friend were in the process of picking up the area at the foot of the steps. The built-in bookshelf along the wall had emptied itself of all the books in the attack on the weretigers. I recognized Rose's companion from the wake a few days earlier.

"Hi, I'm Chip."

"Warren," he replied. He held out a hand.

I shook it, noting his firm, calloused grip. "I saw you here after the funeral."

"I'm a long-time family friend. Rose and I go way back."

"His family are loyal retainers of our line dating back to the old country," Rose added as she passed by with a stack of books in her arms.

"It's a pleasure to meet you, Warren. I guess this whole magical world thing is old hat to you."

He shrugged. "I grew up with it. It's all normal to me."

That set me wondering what kind of retainer he was. Did he have powers, too?

He must've caught me studying him. "I'm a werewolf. Rose and I went through school together."

"Magic school?"

Rose laughed. "No, we went to regular schools just like you. The tough part was keeping our true natures hidden from the other kids, though. We were always different, and they picked up on it. That left us alone to be friends with each other."

Warren nodded. "Kids pick up on things that human adults have forgotten how to recognize. Their parents ignore them when they point out one of us. It's helpful in keeping the veil in place between the two worlds."

"I guess it is." I looked back and forth between them and said, "So, uh, are you two an item?"

"Oh, gods no," Rose said. Her light-hearted laugh lit up the room. "Not that Warren didn't try when we were younger."

He winced. "She shut me down just as forcefully then, too. It wasn't pretty."

"Ouch," I said. "You had a salty edge to you even back then, didn't you Rose?"

"I am who I am. I've never pretended to be anything else. Now you two stop gabbing and help me clean up things here. I'd like to finish before dawn."

I knelt down and started gathering books, thinking about why I'd asked if they were together. What did I care? Rose and I had our fling. We both knew after that episode it would never work out between us.

With three of us digging into the cleanup, it didn't take us long to finish up. I brought a bucket of water and placed it on the carpet in front of the sofa. I pulled out a sponge and started blotting at the large bloodstain on the floor. Every now and then I'd wring out the sponge in the water, turning it a darker shade of pink with every pass. The work lightened the stain from deep crimson to a faded pink.

Rose came in from the kitchen with a pair of coffee mugs. "You're never going to get that out completely. You'll have to replace it."

Warren remarked from where he stood rearranging the books on the shelves, "You could just buy an area rug and cover it up. Much easier than cleaning it. Take it from me, blood is hard to get out of any fabric."

"I'm more worried about Sadie's reaction to it. I don't want her asking about the bloodstains on the floor. I plan on getting it replaced, but that'll take some time."

"He's loaded, Warren. He can afford to buy this whole house several times over without blinking an eye."

"My money isn't the issue here. It's about keeping a four-year-old from seeing the blood splatter from an impaled monster in her family room. She sits right there when she watches her shows on the TV." I pointed at the sofa next to the stain.

"Here," Rose said, handing me one of the mugs. "Take a break. I put one of the casseroles in the oven. You need some food after all the work and the adrenaline rush of last night. The food will help restore your mana levels, too."

"Thanks." I dropped the sponge in the bucket and took the mug from her. I took a sip. Black, just the way I liked it. I lifted the mug in thanks and sipped again.

Warren came over, sniffed at the coffee in the air, and headed to the kitchen. Rose watched him go and said, "We need to plan for what's next. The two weretigers are still out there. I'm sure they're not going to give up."

"What do they have against the kids? I thought all we had to worry about was the other Fae."

"They're hired muscle. We do have to worry about the other Fae, along with all the people they hire to come after us. Most of the Fae nobility don't like to get their hands dirty. They prefer to pull the levers of power instead."

"If that's the case, what happened to you and your branch of the family?" I smiled as I said it. I knew Rose was an active adventurer in her own right. It made me wonder if her "archeological digs" were actually much more than that.

"I trained in the martial arts at an early age once I learned I wasn't in line to bear the Queen. I figured I could make myself useful in other ways. In our branch of the family, the second children were expected to become warriors. It's a holdover from a much more war-like time many centuries ago."

"So that's what awaits Addy when he grows up, too?"

"If he wants. He'll have a choice in the end, but I'll make sure he learns to defend himself along the way."

"What about Sadie? She should learn to fight, too."

"I'll teach her," Rose said. "But she needs to learn so much more. There's a rich history associated with our family and its responsibilities. She must learn our place in the Fae hierarchy and how to manage the loyalty of the others once she ascends to the throne."

"Sounds like business and politics. I can help her with that." That all sounded exciting to me.

"Are you sure you'll still be around?" Rose asked.

"I'm not going anywhere, though I have to ask again if it wouldn't make sense to move them to a more secure location. My penthouse in New York is very secure. I'd like to see these weretigers try to break in there."

"Oh," Rose said. "You think your doorman is up to stopping a pair of angry weretigers who want to get into your building? I told you the kids have to stay here. This is their home, and this is where their protection is the strongest."

"I can protect them wherever they are."

"So can I."

I realized I'd turned to face her. My fists were clenched at my sides so hard, my knuckles started aching.

Rose stood rigid, glaring at me from the opposite side of the couch.

Warren stepped between us. "Hey, hey, let's keep in mind why we're here. The kids, remember?"

I forced myself to relax, flexing my fingers to get the tingles in my hands to go away.

Rose glared at me for a second longer then looked away. She stalked back into the kitchen.

"She doesn't understand what these kids mean to me," I said to Warren.

"Maybe she feels the same way. She wasn't around when the attack against Lili and Bobby came. She was in Central Iraq tracking some rare magical artifact. I know she has a lot of guilt about that."

I knew there had to be more to Rose's archeological adventures than met the eye, especially after the revelation of the Unusual world to me. I hadn't known she wasn't here when the accident— no, it wasn't an accident, when the attack came. I couldn't hold that against her, could I? I hadn't been around much lately either. Maybe if I had, Bobby would have felt comfortable confiding in me about his life with Lili and her family.

"There's plenty of guilt to go around, I guess." I glanced at the closed door to the kitchen. "She still should've told me about the defenses here in the house."

"I'll let the two of you sort that out. I'm just an investigator for hire. I'll keep doing what I can to uncover who was behind their deaths. You two have the much harder job of keeping life moving forward for those kids upstairs. I don't envy you that task. It's a long time until Sadie is old enough to take up the mantle of Queen."

"Will you keep me in the loop of your findings, too? I feel like I should be included more in finding out what happened."

"I'll have to run it past her," Warren hooked a thumb over his shoulder towards the kitchen. "But if she says yes, I have no problem with it."

"No problem with what?" Rose asked, returning to the room.

"I asked Warren to be included in the investigation. I'm the big, bad Guardian for the kids now. I should know what's going on, too."

Rose shrugged. "If that's what you want, fine. But that door swings both ways, Chip. You need to let me know all your plans for the kids. I have to know where they are at all times."

Given what had happened when Lili and Bobby died, I understood her need to feel close to the kids. I could tell her most of what I had been thinking about. She didn't have to know about everything, though. That could come in time.

"Sure, Rose. I'll keep in touch with you about the kids."

With the uneasy truce settled between us, the conversation fell away, leaving an awkward silence.

Warren pulled his phone from his pocket and flipped through it. "Look, I'll leave you two here to take care of the kids. I can get a driver to come get me on the app here."

"No," Rose said. "I can drive you back into town. We're done here."

"What if the weretigers come back?" I asked. "Maybe I should get a gun, with silver bullets?"

"If you want to piss them off," Warren said with a chuckle. "Oh, don't get me wrong. The silver will work, but you'd better be a good shot and drop them with the first round or two. Otherwise, you'll end up with a very angry cat all over your ass."

I pointed at Rose's sword laying across the back of the sofa cushions. "What about something like that? I can't imagine that would be any better."

Rose snorted a laugh. "In the hands of a noob like you, it would be worse than a gun. I've trained all my life to use that sword. Plus, it has very strong magic infused into the blade. Believe me, when I catch up with those weretigers, they're going to find out just how deadly that sword is in my hands."

"I could learn, that's all I'm saying. I've never felt so helpless in my life. Is there someone I could get sword lessons or something like that?"

"Stick with learning what your Guardian powers are," Rose said. "Once you've mastered them, we'll talk about getting you a weapon."

She picked up her sword and pointed it at the kitchen. "We're leaving. They broke in through the back door in there and then left by the front door, I think. I'll text you the names of some contractors you can use to fix the door and jamb. I've put a stronger ward on the entryway that should discourage them if they return. I don't think they will. One of them is wounded and you bested the other. That will sting and take some getting over." She checked her watch. "I set the timer in the kitchen for the casserole. It'll be ready in an hour or so. Make sure you eat some of it before the kids wake up. They're going to be cranky in the morning after last night's action."

Warren headed for the front door and Rose followed him. I watched her go, seeing her in a different light, carrying a sword and searching for magic all over the world for a living. I still had so much to learn about her.

Her advice about getting some sleep was good. I sat on the couch and leaned back staring up at the ceiling for a moment to rest. I fell asleep within a few seconds.

15

Rose

After taking care of the attack on the kids, I dropped Warren off at his apartment and went back to my own place to get some sleep. I maintained an apartment here in Westminster for those times when I wasn't on the road chasing down some magical rumor or another. It was better than always sleeping at either Aunt Allura's or at Lili's.

I woke up feeling refreshed and a little driven to do something about the attack last night. Between the coroner's report Warren had found and the weretigers' attack on the house, I had to believe they were the same ones who'd killed Lili and Bobby.

Warren had said there weren't any weretigers who lived in the area nearby. That meant they were from out of town, probably from Baltimore, or maybe Washington, DC. I decided to travel to Baltimore first. I knew a weretiger there who might talk to me if I approached her right. They were solitary and territorial creatures. With shifters like werewolves you went to the pack leader to deal with a problem. There wasn't a leader like that to go to for tiger kind.

That was true for most of the big cats. The were-jaguars of Central and South America had formed a criminal cartel that dealt with most of the American were-cats. The weretigers didn't consider themselves part of that group and remained aloof from their control.

Those who lived in the region still tended to keep track of any other werecats in their back yards. I hoped my contact would know something about the two who'd attacked the house.

I grabbed a drive-thru iced coffee on the way to Baltimore. It was a forty-five minute drive to get to where I was going, so I had time to think about what Chip had said at the house earlier. I'm sure he'd been terrified during the attack. He'd done well protecting the kids, though. I couldn't argue that. I still didn't think arming him right now was the right choice. His powers were still emerging. If I complicated that with some sort of magical weapon, he might not discover a key skill he'd need to keep Sadie and Addy safe.

It would have to be something I kept in the back of my mind while things developed. It might make sense to find him something eventually, but not right now. I knew a few weapon smiths who might be able to make something that fit Chip's personality. A sword said as much about the person wielding it as it did about its killing ability. That would be something to ponder.

I pulled off the expressway into the city and drove through a few neighborhoods until I reached a broad open park area. It was the Maryland Zoo, my destination. I parked in the lot and went up to the kiosk to purchase my ticket for a day pass, then walked inside. I ignored the animal enclosures, walking straight to the back of the park.

My search initially proved unsuccessful. The person I looked for wasn't where I usually found her on the rare occasions when I'd needed to speak with her. I wandered around the area around her office for a little while, hoping to spot her.

I eventually found her feeding the brown bears. She came walking down a path that led to the back of the bear enclosure. A frown crossed her face as soon as she spotted me.

"I thought I smelled Fae about. It didn't occur to me it might be you, though." The woman who walked up to me looked to be about forty years old with wiry orange curls hanging down from beneath her broad-brimmed hat.

"Hi, Seana, it's been awhile."

"What do you want, Rose? You never come around unless you want something."

"That's not true. I came that one time with my sister and aunt to deliver our family's rather generous contribution to help keep the zoo afloat. Remember?"

"I do, but that was more your aunt's doing than yours. I don't see her here asking me questions."

I bit down my initial urge to flash some Fae power in my eyes. She wouldn't react well to the challenge. Instead, I put on a smile. "Look, this won't take too long. I'll walk with you while you work."

The zookeeper shrugged. "Suit yourself."

"I wondered if you'd heard about any other weretigers in the area?"

She shot me a glance. "Why are you asking?"

I noticed she didn't say no. "There was an attack on my sister's house last night. It was two weretigers. One was injured before they were driven off."

"Your sister's house? I'd heard she was dead along with her husband. Why would someone attack their home. Did she have valuables she kept there?"

I ignored the callous way she handled Lili's death. Her kind didn't see Fae as their superiors. "Just her children. Their human uncle was home when the attack came. He locked them in a safe room until the danger had passed."

Seana pressed her lips together into a firm line. I could tell she didn't like hearing that one of her kind had exposed a human to the Unusual world.

"Look, I just want to find them and convince them to leave whatever they're after alone."

"Bullshit, Rose. You plan on killing them for attacking your family. Don't lie to me. I know who and what you are."

"So, you won't help me?"

"I didn't say that." Seana stopped at a small shed and dropped off the bucket she carried. "If these two newcomers endangered all of us by risking exposure to the human world, I have no pity on them."

"That sounds like you don't know who they are."

"I've heard a few things about two new cats in the area. They haven't been around here. My territory is well marked for those who know what to look for. They wouldn't enter it without permission."

"If they're not friends of yours, then you won't have a problem helping me with a location if you have it."

Seana's piercing golden eyes stared back at me from the shade of her hat's brim.

I held her gaze, realizing neither of us would look away first.

After a few seconds, she nodded. "I'll tell you what little I know. There's a house over in Camden that is a sort of hostel for roaming cats. It's considered safe ground for those of us that are territorial. You have to promise me that you'll not attack them there. Wait until they've left and track them to somewhere else before you go after them."

"I can do that. Safe houses are important for all of us. I'll respect that boundary." I needed her help, and not just now. I would again in the future, I was sure. This wasn't the time to burn any bridges by attacking residents in that location. I'd have to come up with a way to trail them, though. I didn't want to attack them right away. Someone else had hired them and that was almost more important than taking out the threat the weretigers posed at the moment.

She seemed satisfied with my agreement. "I'll text you the address. You still have the same number?"

"Yes. Thank you, Seana. This is about family, and I want to get this resolved."

"As long as you don't violate the safe house, their condition when you're done with them isn't my concern."

I shook her hand and left her to her animals. I couldn't help but wonder if she viewed any of them as prey for her hunting urges. Being a dog person, cat personalities completely evaded my understanding.

Back at the car, I sat in the parking lot thinking about the next move. I could put Warren on it. He'd have to be careful. Most Unusuals had a heightened sense of awareness about their surroundings, and these two subjects would be on their guard after their botched attack. I knew I would be after something like that.

My phone buzzed and I checked the message that came in. It was from Seana. I tapped the address and opened my map application. I figured I'd swing by the safehouse and do a little drive-by recon while I was here in the city. I started the car and left the zoo behind me.

Ten minutes later, I neared the location I was looking for. It was down a side street on the left up ahead. As soon as I turned onto the street, my eyes widened. Halfway down, the area was filled with police cars, an ambulance, and a fire truck. It looked like it was around the location of my destination.

I drove forward until an officer in the street directed me to stop.

"What's your business here, ma'am?"

"I was just cutting through on my way to pick up a friend," I said, putting on my little lost girl face. My eyes flashed with magical energy as I sent a truth suggestion into the cop's mind. "What's happening? I hope it's nothing serious."

He stared at me, trying to decide if he'd seen my eyes light up or not. It only lasted a second, then the spell took hold. His voice became almost sleepy. "Yeah, somebody stuffed two bodies into a small dumpster next to a youth hostel up ahead. It looks like gang activity."

"That's a shame. Were they from around here?"

"Nope, from out of the country. A pair of brothers from Bangladesh. They probably got caught up in the wrong place at the wrong time. They had just arrived in town a few days ago from Philly."

Bangladesh was prime weretiger country. The two dead guys had to be my weretigers. Someone had come here ahead of me, closing off this avenue to track down the person behind Lili's death. I wondered what they'd been doing up in Philly before they came here.

"Thank you, officer. That's all I need to know." I released the charm. "Which way would you like me to proceed?"

He shook his head to clear the fog my spell left in its wake. He wouldn't remember even seeing me. "You'll need to turn down this alley right here and proceed to your friend's on another route."

"Thank you. Have a nice day."

"You, too."

He waved me along and I turned down the alley, craning my neck to see as much as I could between all the vehicles, which wasn't much. I'd have to get Warren to use his contacts to try and pull the incident reports and any other information that made its way into official systems. That was merely to confirm what I already knew. I didn't believe in coincidences. These two were the ones I was looking for.

I'd have to find another way to follow the trail back to who had my sister killed. I pounded my clenched fist on the top of the steering wheel. Whoever had done this, must've been waiting here for them to return from their attack. They had either already planned on killing them to cover their tracks, or they didn't like the answers they got about the attack's failure. Either way, it was an indication of the relative power of whoever it was I was after. Killing two weretigers, even if one was injured, was no small feat.

I pulled over long enough to text Seana a quick message about what I'd found. I wanted to make sure she knew it wasn't me who'd killed them. Once the message was sent, I drove across the Inner Harbor district and hopped onto the expressway back out of the city. This had been a big dead end and left me with more questions than answers. I had a feeling time wasn't on my side. Another attack would be coming. I was going to have to drive up to Philadelphia and spend a few days up there tracking down what the two dead goons had been doing there before they came south. It might tell me who had contacted them to come to Baltimore.

16

Chip

The few days after the attack marked a return to some sort of normal, though I was still learning the routine. I was able to clean up the mess from what was left of Sadie's door and have a local handyman come by to install and paint a new one to match the one that had been broken. He tried to find out what had happened to the old door, but I hinted that I'd pay a little extra if he kept his questions to himself. That shut him up.

While that work was going on and the kids were occupied with playing or napping, I was able to set up several conference calls with Eddie and some key institutional investors for the new fund with minimal interruptions from the kids. I knew it wasn't optimal and Eddie reminded me about the need to show up on the relevant news show soon.

Rose had told me she was heading out of town for a little bit and that she'd arranged for some alternative protection while she was gone. I had no idea what that meant, but if it meant she stayed out of my hair for a bit, then I could proceed with the next part of my plan to fit into this Guardian role my brother had left for me.

I'd reached out to a friend in New York who handled high-end household help for several investment banking people I knew. They all had raved about her placements. She sent me several resumes of potential nannies for hire. After several video interviews on the computer, I'd settled on seeing one of them in person. She was taking a gap year before college and had been babysitting for several prominent families since she was thirteen. She had first aid and CPR training, too. I figured I could handle anything else she needed to know.

She was coming by this morning for a final interview and to spend some time with the kids to see how they liked her. I hoped it worked out. This would free me up to do everything I needed to do to get this fund launched.

The doorbell rang soon after I'd finished cleaning up the kids from breakfast. I picked up Addy and went to see if it was Cassidy, the nanny. Sadie followed along behind me. She'd been very clingy since the attack. It was something I understood, but which left me with even less time than was optimal. Hopefully, I could transfer her clinginess to the new helper.

I opened the door to be greeted by a tall redhead with a pixie cut and a beaming smile. She had several interesting shapes tattooed on her forearms, including an intricate five-pointed star design, but I wasn't the sort that was bothered by tats on a woman. I appreciated body art on the female form in general.

"Mr. Proctor," she said, extending her hand. "It's a pleasure to meet you in person."

I shook her hand and stepped back to wave her into the home. "It's nice to see you in the flesh, too. It was so nice of you to be willing to travel down here for the day."

"I couldn't turn down a first-class plane ticket and free accommodations in the city for a few days. Thank you for your generosity." She stepped past me into the house.

I shut the door once she was inside. She had a stuffed hiker's backpack over her shoulders. "It's not a big deal. I'm hoping you won't have to return right away. If this interview works out and you want to get started, I can arrange to have a mover pick up your things and bring what you need down from New York."

Cassidy smiled. "I travel light. I have everything I need in my pack." She knelt down, sliding the pack from her shoulders and leaning it against the coat closet door. "And who do we have here? My name is Cassie."

Sadie, who'd been standing behind me with her little arms wrapped around my knees peeked around me. "I'm Sadie. You look funny. Why are you all red?"

I flushed with embarrassment. "I'm so sorry, I don't know where that came from."

"Don't worry about it," Cassidy said, chuckling a little. "Kids are very direct." She looked at Sadie. "I'm red because that's how I was born. Do you like my red hair? I think it makes me special."

"I wish I had red hair. I want to be special, too. Can I get red hair, Uncle Chip?"

"Um, we'll see about that another time. Why don't we spend some time getting to know Cassidy first."

"She said her name is Cassie, Uncle Chip."

I laughed. "So she did, Sadie. I'll keep that in mind from now on."

Sadie seemed to have overcome her shyness. She reached out and grabbed Cassie's hand. "Come on. Let me show you my toys."

Cassie stopped only to reach out for Addison. I handed her the baby, who cooed and gurgled at the newcomer.

"Ooo, aren't you just the cutest. Okay, Sadie. Let's go see your toys."

I watched them move across the living room and into the family room area where the corner filled with toys was located. Cassie sat down on the floor with Addy settled in her lap. She and Sadie began a very interesting game of pretend with some of the little people and a doll house.

Seeing that Cassie seemed to be doing alright, I went over to the dining room table and sat down with my laptop. This was my chance to get caught up on the morning's emails. The first up was from my partner, Eddie. He needed some biographical information for our brochures. Rather than answer by email, I popped in my Bluetooth earpiece and dialed him up.

"Dude," Eddie said as soon as he picked up. "You must be psychic. I was just thinking of you."

"I saw your email and wanted to see what you needed the bio for. I have one of those on the website already."

"Yeah, but Ed Greenly from Business Weekly noticed you hadn't been seen around town and wanted to know what you were up to. When I told him, he actually got excited. He thought it would make a great fluff piece to promote the launch. You know, 'Mr. Mom of the Business World' kind of thing. We'd need to include some pics of you and the kids together, but we can have a local photographer take those if you can't come up here in time."

I thought about the article idea. It made me smile. "That might be a great angle, actually. Things are looking up here in the kid department, too."

"Oh, did the new nanny arrive? Is she as cute as her picture? I bet you end up nailing her."

"Yes, she's here." Thank God she couldn't hear him.

Cassie looked over when she heard me talking and smiled.

I nodded at her and said, "She looks like she'll work out great with the kids. Time will tell."

"Yeah," Eddie said. "Time will tell how long it takes you. Maybe I should start an office pool. I know everyone will want to get in on this one."

"Stop it, Eddie. Besides, I have Mia right now and that's just fine with me. I'll look around here for a photographer to shoot some quick pics for the spread. When are they looking to do the piece?"

"He said he can get it in this week's issue if we hurry up. Some other item they had must've gotten pulled."

"Perfect, that'll give us the exposure we need right before the big push."

Cassie and Sadie came over to the table where I was working. "Hold on a sec, Eddie. Did you need something, Cassie?"

"Mr. Proctor, is it alright if we go outside and play a little? The kids could use some fresh air and Sadie wants to show me the swingset and castle in the back yard."

"Sure, you have the run of the house while you're here for this test run. Let's kick all the tires as it were."

She smiled and returned to pick up Addy and then Sadie took her free hand and led them all out back.

"Ooo, Mr. Proctor, can you take a look at my boo-boo?" Eddie said. I could hear his leering tone clearly through the phone.

"You're a sick puppy, Eddie."

"I gotta live vicariously through you and your antics, my friend. My money's on no more than seven days and you'll cave. Mia's up here in New York after all. That's a long way off when there's someone right there in the house."

"I'm ending this call. Email me if you have anything important to say. I'll send you the pics once I find someone to shoot them."

"Sounds good. I'll reach out if anything else comes up."

Eddie disconnected on his end and my thoughts lingered for a few seconds on his lurid suggestions. I shook them off. I had a strict policy regarding keeping business relationships professional. That included nannies, I decided.

Putting that line of thought from my mind, I started a search on my laptop for local photographers. A few popped up that looked promising, but I'd have to see if they could clear the calendar to come over and shoot the pics this afternoon. That was essential to get them up to Ed Greenly at BW right away.

The first two I called didn't pick up. I left voicemails and kept going. I couldn't afford to wait for a callback. The third picked up the phone right away.

"Red Robin Family Photography, I'm Kathy, what can I do for you?"

"Hi, I'm visiting from New York and a national publication needs some photos shot today of me and my niece and nephew. I don't suppose you're available and would be able to turn around the photographs in time for publication later this week?"

"You're in luck. I had a cancellation today. I was supposed to do some graduation photos, but she woke up with a stomach bug. And I can definitely get the photos out in time."

"Excellent. Well, for me, not for her. Could you come over soon? I'm in the Rolling Fields development north of town."

"I can be there in a few hours if that'll give you time to get ready, Mr…"

"I'm Chip, Chip Proctor. That will be fine. Let's say noon. That'll give me time to get the kids cleaned up and ready. If this is your cell, I'll text you the address when we get off this call."

"That would be perfect, Chip. I'll look forward to seeing you and getting these pics shot for you."

She hung up and I texted her the address. She confirmed she got it right away, which I appreciated. I'd have to keep her in mind for any future photography needs I might have in the future. I supposed I'd be expected to do one of those family Christmas card photos later this year. If I had to do it, I could at least get a pro to shoot the picture.

I looked up and out the back window. Cassie had strapped Addy in the baby swing shaped like a red plastic rocket ship. She alternated between pushing him and then Sadie in the swing beside him. Judging from Sadie's grin and the fact that Addy wasn't crying, things looked to be going smoothly.

My phone pinged me with the sound that indicated a VIP email had come in. I checked and saw it was Ed Greenly reaching out with the information for the photo shoot. He wanted to line up a video call later that day to do the accompanying interview. I replied back that would be perfect and told him I'd have the photos for the spread soon.

Taking advantage of Cassie taking care of the kids, I turned to my laptop and dove into work. There was a lot I had let slide by the wayside since I'd come down to take care of the kids. I wanted to put a dent in the to-do list before lunchtime. Then I could tell Cassie she had the job and ask her if she could start right away. Judging from her earlier comments to me, that wouldn't be a problem.

I quickly got lost in the work and didn't look up until I heard Cassie bringing the kids inside. She had a sound asleep Addy in her arms.

"I'm going to take him up and put him down for a nap."

I started to get up. "Let me show you where everything is up there."

"I can do it, Uncle Chip. I'm Cassie's big girl helper."

"Yes, you are," I replied and sat back down. I looked up at Cassie. "Let me know if you need anything."

"I will, Mr. Proctor. The kids are great."

She walked off and I couldn't help but notice how hot she was. That short red hair was a turn on by itself. But, contrary to what Eddie thought, I had a strict "don't shit where you work" policy. It wasn't like I couldn't find someone else if I wanted to. Cassidy was off-limits as far as I was concerned.

Shaking my head at the shame of it all, I went back to my work. There was a lot to get done before the photographer arrived.

17

Rose

It had been a long five days in Philadelphia. I'd tracked down every lead I could find to see where the two dead weretigers had come from. The one thing I could be sure of was they hadn't interacted much at all with the Philly Unusual community while they'd stayed there. In fact, if I hadn't been able to confirm with a former landlord that the two had rented a place there over the last year, I would have thought the original information about their location was wrong.

Whoever had hired them had wanted them to keep a low profile and it seemed they had done that right up until they botched the attack on the house. The mistake, though, had earned them a death sentence from the one who had hired them. Unfortunately, there was no record of who it was who'd originally contacted them. For all I knew it was a clan of local Fae nobility from Bangladesh. I hoped that wasn't the case. I had no experience or contacts in that country.

At the end of my list of options, I went down to the hotel lobby to check out of my room and head back to Maryland. Maybe Warren had better luck there than I did up in Philly. As I stood in line waiting to see the desk clerk, I glanced over at the small newspaper stand by the gift shop.

I froze. What was Sadie doing on the cover of a news magazine? I couldn't wrap my head around what I was seeing. Then realization set in, and anger boiled up inside me.

"That fucking idiot."

The woman in front of me turned to glare at me. I ignored her and continued to stare at the rack of newspapers.

There, on the cover of Business Weekly, was a beaming Charles Henderson Proctor with Addy in one arm and Sadie standing beside him. The headline read *Mr. Mom Fund Manager Talks Work/Life Balance.*

Seething inside and barely able to speak for fear the string of expletives roiling in my brain would spill out, I pulled the plastic keycard out of my pocket and jumped the line to slap it down on the counter. "Room ten-thirty-four. Email the receipt to my account on file."

The woman I'd jumped past, shouted "Hey!" at me, but I was already gone.

I ran for the elevator and my Firebird parked in the underground garage. I was going to kill him. How could he be so stupid? There was no way he'd missed the part I'd said about the family being in hiding and trying to keep a low profile.

The answer was, he hadn't missed it. He'd just ignored it and done whatever Chip wanted to do because that's who Chip was. As soon as I was in the car and heading for I-95 to head south, I dialed up Warren on my phone.

"What's up, Rose? I still haven't uncovered anything new, if that's why you're calling."

"Have you seen the cover of the latest Business Weekly?"

"No," he said, a chuckle in his voice. "It's not really on the top of my reading list. You should know that."

"Well, I want you to drive around town and buy every copy you find. Start at the places closest to my aunt's home. Make sure you hit every convenience store that might have a newsstand inside."

"What's this all about?"

"You'll see when you start buying them up. Get to it and call me back when you're finished. Bill me for the cost in your next invoice. I'm on my way back and should be there in a few hours."

"Any luck up in Philly?"

"No, they were definitely here, but it's a dead end. We'll have to try to figure some other way to track down their boss. I'll fill you in when I get there. For now, you've got work to do."

I cut off the call before he could answer, anger still ruling my emotions. Chip had stepped over a line with this. Despite the warnings to the contrary, he'd gone and put the kids on the front page of a national publication. I could almost hear his objections rattling off the reasons why I was overreacting. An image popped into my head of me throttling him in the backyard with the swing set in the background just like in the photograph on the cover. To anyone else, it might have seemed amusing. For me it was planning ahead.

The trip south didn't go the way I'd planned at all. Traffic on I-95 was busier than usual, and I got caught up in several backups because serious accidents had the road closed. In each of those cases, I was caught between exits and couldn't get off the highway to take a detour. The normal two-and-a-half-hour trip took almost seven hours by the time I rolled into Westminster.

The repeated delays only served to fuel my anger and gave me ample time to play out the way I intended for the confrontation to play out. This kind of selfish shenanigans was exactly what I'd warned my sister about when she'd first chosen him as the Guardian. I'd repeated those warnings to my aunt, too, after Lili died.

No one had listened to me.

By the time I arrived in Westminster, my seething anger had cooled to a severe frostiness driven by the need to make sure everything was right before I confronted Chip. I called Warren and he met me outside my apartment building in the parking lot. He got out of his beat-up sedan and popped the trunk. Bundled copies of Business Weekly filled it.

Seeing Chip's smiling face staring up at me from the top copy almost set me off again. I tamped down my anger and asked, "Did you get all of them?"

"All that weren't already sold. I have no way of knowing who might have a copy." He fell silent for a second then felt the need to fill the void. "It's a really good picture of the kids."

"What are you talking about? I don't care if they looked cute or not. I care that their faces are plastered all across the country right now for anyone who has a grudge against the family to come find us."

"How?" Warren asked.

"What do you mean, 'how?' The pictures are right there."

"No, I mean how will they connect the kids to you and your family? The whole article is about Chip. There's a few mentions of the kids but no details of who they are, just that he's their legal guardian. It's all about him. There's nothing to even connect it to Lili and Bobby."

I hadn't read the article and I chewed my lip, trying not to bite Warren's head off. He had a point. "There's still someone out there who knows exactly who the kids are, though. This could be seen as a taunt after their attack on the house. It could spur another stronger attack."

"You know if they want to attack the kids, they'll do it or not, based on what they want." When I glared at him, Warren held up his hands in surrender. "Look, I'm just the messenger here. I did what you wanted me to do. Now what are we supposed to do with all these magazines?"

"Drive over there, we'll throw them all into the recycling dumpster." I walked across the parking lot and waited for Warren to bring his car over so we could empty his trunk.

With every magazine I tossed into the dumpster, I saw Chip's smiling face looking up at me. When I was finished with him later, I was going to save a copy and go right to Aunt Allura. I was right to get them off the newsstands and keep her from seeing them before I'd fixed the problem. Now I could show her what happened and how I'd solved the problem the right way.

Warren closed the trunk lid. "Where are you going now?"

"To have a little chat with Chip. He should be getting the kids dinner about now. It'll be a good time to talk with him, so I don't blow up completely in front of the kids."

"Good luck with that. I'll send you a bill for the time today and the cost of the magazines." He drove off leaving me in the parking lot.

I took some deep, cleansing breaths as I drove to Lili's house. By the time I got there, I found I had become almost calm. I pulled up out front and noticed Chip's car wasn't in the driveway. It was getting on towards dusk and dinner time. I figured he had taken the kids somewhere for food.

I texted him to see where he was.

Out to dinner. Talk later.

Oh, hell no. *Nope, talk now. Where are you?*

Johannsen's downtown. It can wait until later.

I couldn't believe he'd taken the kids out to a fancy restaurant, especially by himself. *You took the kids there for dinner?*

No. Kids are with the nanny. I'm with Mia.

I almost threw the phone onto the sidewalk beside the car. A nanny! He'd lost his mind. I ran up to the house and used my key to let myself in.

"Sadie, honey, are you here?"

There was no answer. The only light on was the one leading up the stairs.

"Sadie, answer me honey." I checked all the rooms, ending in her bedroom, I even looking under the bed to see if Bernard was there. He wasn't. A bed troll only manifested when their charge was in the room at nighttime.

I pulled out my phone and rang Chip.

"Rose, this can wait until later. I'm busy."

"Where. Are. The kids. Chip?"

The annoyed response came instantly. "They're home."

"They're gone."

"What do you mean they're gone?" Shock started to register in Chip's tone.

"I mean I'm at the house and no one is home. You said they're with the nanny. Where's that?"

"She should have them at the house. Maybe she took them to the playground down the street."

"Nope, I passed it on the way here. I would've seen them. Come home now. I'm calling for some help to locate them."

Chip started to say something, but I cut him off and hung up. I called Warren.

"Yeah, Rose." He didn't sound happy. He obviously thought he was finished for the evening.

"Did you know Chip hired a nanny?"

"No, I would've told you. Who did he hire?"

"No idea," I said. "I bet he has no idea of who he hired either. He's on his way back to the house now. He was out to dinner and left the kids alone with this new nanny."

"What do you want me to do?"

"Stay close to the phone and be ready to run a background check through all your channels. It might be something innocent. I don't think it is, but I'll hope for the best."

"I'll be here."

After Warren got off the phone, I went downstairs and checked the rest of the house for any clue of where they might be. After a quick search I discovered the stroller was gone along with the baby carrier that attached to it. Sadie's red jacket with a hood was gone, too. Maybe they were at the park after all.

I decided I had time to check before Chip got home. I drove through the neighborhood to the playground next to the elementary school. There were other families there with their kids. There was no sign of Sadie and Addison, though.

I drove back to the house, taking my time to check the side streets in case they were just out for a walk. Chip's Tesla was in the driveway when I got back.

I parked and ran inside. He stood with Mia and had his phone pressed to his ear.

"Cassie, this is Mr. Proctor. You didn't say you were going out. I'm home and don't know where you are with the kids. Call me right away."

He hung up and shot me a look, his brow furrowed with worry.

"Who's Cassie? I assume she's the nanny you hired after I told you not to."

"She's fully vetted and came highly recommended. I'm sure she's in a bad service area or something. I've texted and called her. She'll call back as soon as she gets the message."

I fought down the scream of rage about to escape me and kept my voice completely level. "Who vetted her, Chip? Not me. I know that much because she never would have passed. You're the Guardian, not her."

"Exactly, Rose. I'm the Guardian. That means I make the decisions. I chose to hire some help just like any normal single parent would."

"You're not a normal single parent, you idiot."

Mia moved between us as tempers heated for both of us. "Let's just calm down here. I'm sure there's a perfectly reasonable explanation for this. Is there some way you can track her phone, honey?"

I cursed the fact that Mia came up with the idea first. "Chip, give me her number. Warren can track it if she's got it turned on." I waited while he texted me the contact information. I forwarded it to Warren and told him to track its location right away.

"He'll find her general location if she's stupid enough to leave it on. It's probably a burner anyway."

Chip shook his head. "She's really quite nice. I'm positive there's nothing going on here but a misunderstanding."

"Look outside, Chip. It's getting dark. It's the kids' bedtime soon. She should be here doing the bath and bedtime thing. Where is she?"

"I don't—" Chip fumbled with the answer and looked out through the front window at the darkening sky. "I don't know, okay?"

Mia came over and hugged herself close to Chip's arm. "You didn't do anything wrong, honey. I'm sure it'll all work out. No one would harm those kids. Who would do such a thing?"

Judging from her reaction, Chip hadn't told her the truth. She had no idea what was really going on here.

"Mia," I said. "Would you give Chip and I a few minutes to talk about some delicate family business? Maybe you could go and make some coffee while we chat?"

The supermodel looked to Chip for an okay and when he nodded, she sniffed and left with her nose in the air.

I waited until she was all the way in the kitchen with the door shut before I started talking again. I forced myself to keep my voice low.

"Chip, you can sense the kids. You know where Sadie is right now. You just forgot. Use your power to find her."

"I hadn't thought of that. I didn't feel any fear or pain. I don't think she's in any danger or I'd know it."

"That just means she trusts whoever she's with. Just concentrate on Sadie and tell me what you feel."

He closed his eyes and lifted his chin a little like he was listening to something. He stayed like that for almost a full minute, turning first this way and then back the other way like he was tuning an antenna.

His eyes popped open, and he pointed to the Northwest. "That way. And it's very faint, like a distant echo of what I usually feel."

"That means they're getting farther away. She probably put them in her car."

"She doesn't have a car."

"What about Lili's minivan?" I asked.

We both ran into the kitchen and through the garage door. It was empty. Lili's minivan was gone.

"Come on, Chip." I tugged at his arm.

"Where are we going?"

I pointed to the street through the window at my car. "We're following that minivan."

Mia stood by the coffee maker in the kitchen listening to our strange discussion. "Maybe I should stay here in case they come home while you're gone."

"Good idea," we both said at the same time.

Chip glared at me for telling his girlfriend what to do. He turned to her. "You keep the lights on, and I'll keep in touch by phone. We shouldn't be that long. This is all a misunderstanding."

I didn't agree with him. I had a bad feeling about this, but I kept my thoughts to myself.

"I'll drive, Chip, so you can navigate. Come on."

We left and climbed into the Firebird. I left a double strip of rubber on the street outside the home as we drove away.

18

Chip

The sensation in the back of my mind when I focused on Sadie was sort of like that tickle at the back of your throat that wasn't quite enough to make you cough. I could make out her general direction, but she was too far away to get a good sense of how she was or what she was feeling. It worried me, but I didn't tell Rose.

"Which way, Chip?" Rose asked as she approached an intersection.

I pointed to the right and she swerved onto the shoulder to go around the cars stopped at the light. She took the turn without slowing at all, cutting off a pickup truck coming through the intersection. The driver leaned on the horn and gave us a one-finger salute for good measure.

When we turned, I concentrated on where Sadie was. She seemed to be off to the right again and I pointed at the exit that took us up and onto the road to Gettysburg.

"How far away are the kids?"

"What? How should I know?"

"You can sense them, right? How close are they?"

I shrugged. "I can sense Sadie mostly. Addy not so much. She's too far off to pick up on her emotions, though. I can usually tell if she's happy or sad. Right now, I'm getting nothing but a distant sense of direction."

"Keep trying." Rose stomped on the gas and drove around a panel van, nearly running a car coming in the opposite direction off the road.

I clutched at the dashboard. "We aren't going to do them any good if we're dead, Rose."

"I'm driving. We won't die. Just tell me if we're getting any closer or if the direction changes."

"I don't understand what Cassie was thinking. I can't figure out where she's going."

Rose gave a derisive snort. "You act like she's just out for a jaunt with the kids. She's kidnapped them, Chip, and it's all your fault."

I wracked my brain, trying to look for any indication that Cassie was something more than a woman trying to make extra cash for college as a nanny just like she'd said. As a nanny, she'd been perfect from the start and Eddie had said she came with great recommendations from numerous people up in New York. The nanny network up there was solid. There's no way she could've faked that.

"There has to be a reasonable explanation, Rose. None of this makes any sense."

"Chip, when this is all done and over with, I'm going to school you in some hard lessons about the Unusual world. Rule one is *nothing is what it seems*."

"You sure weren't," I mumbled under my breath.

"I heard that." Rose didn't take her eyes off the road as she said it, swerving in a smooth curve around another car ahead of us.

The road wasn't a major highway, just a two-lane road. There weren't many opportunities to pass the slower traffic in front of us. She took advantage of the openings that came up, though.

It wasn't long before we got close to the Pennsylvania state line. I pointed at a road sign with the distance to towns ahead of us. "If she keeps going this way, she'll be in Gettysburg soon. The feeling of direction is the same, but the sensation is definitely getting stronger. We're catching up."

"That, or she's stopped with the kids at her destination already."

"I don't think she's going to hurt them, Rose."

She shot me a glance before turning her attention back to the road ahead. "What makes you say that? She's stolen them from us."

"Yeah, but if she wanted to hurt them, she's had plenty of opportunities this week to be alone with them and do that."

"How long has she been here?"

"Five days."

"So, you hired her as soon as I left town. Hired her right after the attack on the house, too. Didn't that teach you anything?"

"She didn't have anything to do with that. She was in New York. She's not some cat monster."

"Do you know what weretigers look like when they're not shifted into their man-tiger form?"

I shook my head.

"They look like normal people. They look like everyday nannies and shopkeepers and plumbers and everyone else. You can't tell them apart from anyone else unless you know the signs to look for."

I thought about it, trying to think of what Rose meant. "What kind of signs would you look for exactly?"

"It could be anything. Most Unusuals have something that marks them. Some have tattoos or other types of markings that tell you what they are."

"Everyone has tattoos, Rose. You have one. Remember, I got to see it at the wedding reception."

"Does Cassie have tattoos, Chip?"

"Yeah, but so does every other eighteen-year-old out there."

"Describe them to me," Rose said.

I tried to remember what the tattoos looked like. Most were on her forearms and weren't easy to describe. "Most were just intricate designs. One was of a star inside a circle with more of the blocky designs around it."

Rose pounded her fist on the top of the steering wheel. "You idiot. I can't believe you actually hired a witch to watch the kids."

"How'd you get to witch based on what I just told you? It could be completely harmless. It was just a tattoo."

"You just described a pentagram on her arm surrounded by runes,

Chip. They're put there when she comes into her powers. You hired a witch to be nanny to your niece and nephew. How could you be so stupid?"

"She's not a witch, Rose. I'm sure of it." As soon as I said it, I knew it sounded hollow. The evidence against Cassie was mounting. She had absolutely no reason to take the kids anywhere tonight. The fact that she was running out of state was indictment enough.

We crossed the line into Pennsylvania and soon after that, hit the area around the Gettysburg National Battlefield. I felt a pull to the side and pointed to the left.

"There! We're getting closer. I can feel Sadie's emotions a little. She's sad and scared."

"Of course she is. There's a witch out there planning to do gods know what with her and Addy."

I started calling out turns on country roads running through the battlefield, acting as a human GPS system as I homed in on Sadie's position. We ended up on a road called Sickles Avenue.

"Slow down. We're close." I looked around and then pointed to a monument lit up in our headlights ahead. It was a large bronze Celtic cross mounted on a stone base jutting up twenty feet in the air. "There, pull over by the monument."

Something about the monument pulled at me. I got out and walked over to the monument. I shined my phone flashlight on the base. It was the monument to the Union Army's Irish Brigade, which fought in the battle near this location.

I turned in place, shining my flashlight around looking for any sign of Sadie and Addison. I spotted Lili's minivan pulled into the trees off the road just beyond the monument.

Rose saw the van, too. "They're here somewhere. Where are they, Chip? Shut off that light and trust your new senses. Where's Sadie?"

I shut off the phone light, plunging my eyes into the encroaching darkness of the trees around us. Then I felt the pull to Sadie again. At the same time, I realized I could see better, the darkness pulling back wherever I focused my gaze just like it had back during the weretiger attack. "I can tell she's close and I can see in the dark now. I forgot to tell you about that. It's a little like tunnel vision. My peripheral vision is just as blind in the dark, but when I stare into the night, it sort of pulls away and reveals what's hidden."

"That's dark-sight. It's a rare magical skill. Your Guardian powers are growing."

I looked Rose's way, seeing her lit up in the surrounding darkness holding her shining sword at her side.

"You're going to stab her with that? Isn't that overkill? She's just a teenager."

"No, Chip, she just looks like a teenager. There's no telling how old she really is. She will be a formidable opponent. Her magic was strong enough to get through my wards and past your Guardian senses without setting off any alarms." She pointed to the woods. "Lead the way. We're running out of time."

I ran into the trees behind the monument, weaving my way between the trunks. The sense of Sadie in the back of my mind became stronger with each step.

Voices filtered through from up ahead and I slowed my pace, trying to hear what they were saying. Rose slowed behind me as well. I recognized one of them right away. It was Cassie. The other voices were male and had an Irish lilt to them.

One of the men said, "This wasn't part of the bargain, witch. You asked us to help you cast a glamour to control a Fae noble. This is a little girl."

"I told you I could help you find the eternal rest you sought," Cassie said. "You agreed to help me. You can't go back on the bargain now."

"But she's a mere lass, not an evil Fae from the old country," another of the male voices said. "You're not telling us something."

"She will grow to be a Fae of great power and influence. You all know from the old stories what power the Fae can hold over ordinary folk who aren't protected. The glamour you help me cast will allow me to control her as she grows and stop her from exerting her full power."

The first male voice said. "You're not telling us the whole story, girlie. There's something else going on here."

There was a flash of red light ahead through the trees. Cassie shouted. "You will obey me and fulfill the bargain we made. I possess the power to damn your souls to hell as easily as I can send you to your final rest. Which will it be?"

Sadie cried out in pain, a pain I felt through our link. I reacted on pure instinct. My arms stretched out in front of me as I ran, my palms facing forward. I had to get to Sadie as fast possible.

I broke into a circular clearing in the trees. Cassie stood to the left. The baby carrier with Addy sat on the ground by her feet. She gripped Sadie's arm, pulling the arm up over her head at an awkward angle.

"Let her go!" As the last word left my mouth, I thrust outward with my will through my hands. I'd never done anything like this before, but I figured I could use my defensive shield as an offensive weapon of sorts, too.

Cassie dropped Sadie as the force hit her. Her eyes went wide as she flew backward and slammed into a large oak tree behind her. She slid down the trunk and slumped to the ground. A groan escaped her as she struggled to rise to her feet.

Five glowing pale white figures stood nearby, and I turned my attention on them, and I ran over and scooped up Sadie with one hand and grabbed Addy's carrier with the other. The figures wore uniforms and caps straight out of an American Civil War reenactment.

I stared at them ready to thrust out with my will again if they moved any closer than they were. For now, they remained where they were.

Rose entered the clearing behind me and pointed her sword at the witch now standing by the oak. "You're going to regret coming after my niece, witch. I'm going to carve you into bits until you tell me who it was who sent you to do this."

"You'll try," Cassie said. She pointed two fingers of her left hand in a v-shape at Rose. Vines grew up from the ground and wrapped around her legs up to her waist.

"Damn you if you think this is going to hold me." Rose started chopping at the thick vines where they came out of the ground, trying to free herself.

Cassie didn't wait to see if she got free. She glanced one time in our direction and then bolted for the trees. She ran fast and disappeared into the hazy darkness at the edge of my enhanced vision.

Rose finally freed herself and ran past me and the kids. "Stay here." She followed Cassie into the woods.

I knelt down, keeping an eye on the glowing figures nearby. "Sadie, are you alright?"

Two small arms wrapped around my neck and squeezed at me as hard as they could. "Uncle Chip, you found me."

"I will always come and find you, kiddo. Are you injured? Did she hurt you?"

"Just my arm a little," Sadie said, sniffling back tears as she tried to be brave.

"Okay, just stay here by me while I see what these men want."

"They're not men, Uncle Chip. They're ghosts."

"I know that, I just meant— never mind that. I want to talk with them."

I turned my full attention to the five ghosts standing by the far edge of the clearing. "I don't know what you're doing here, but I will protect her with all my power, I promise you."

The leader spoke. He'd been the one arguing with Cassie earlier. "We mean you nor the children any harm. We were misled by the witch to lend her some of our essence for a spell she meant to cast. When we saw who she meant to cast it on, we realized she wasn't being honest with us."

"So, you won't hurt us?" I asked.

Another one, young enough to have been a teen a hundred fifty years before, said, "We just want to stop wandering these woods, reliving our final days over and over again. She promised us rest. Can you help us?"

"I don't think so. I'm still new to this job. My power seems to be focused on protecting my niece and nephew."

Their shoulders slumped in disappointment.

"But I will remember how you helped me save Sadie. You refused to participate in the spell and if I ever discover a way to give you peace, I will come back and do what I can."

The leader nodded. "We can ask for nothing more of you. We are glad you arrived and saved the young ones. You're an honorable man. We will hope and pray for your return."

The leader walked away into the edge of the trees behind the group, followed by the others. Their ghostly forms faded as they left the clearing, leaving me and the children alone.

Sadie laughed and pointed at me. "Uncle Chip, your eyes are glowing blue. I didn't know you had magic, too. It looks funny."

"It must be my night vision magic. I guess I'll have to remember it makes my eyes glow. That might freak ordinary people out if they saw it."

Sadie giggled then snuggled in against me, pulling herself tight to my side.

"Let's sit down here on the soft grass and wait for Aunt Rose to come back. I'm sure she'll be here soon."

Sadie lay down with her head on my lap and dozed while I stroked her hair in the moonlight. Addy let out a baby sigh and continued sleeping as he'd done through the entire event. I hoped Rose wouldn't be too long. I needed to get the kids home.

19

Rose

I tore at the vines wrapped around my legs with my free hand while I hacked at the thick base of the vines around my feet. The sword wasn't the best tool for the job, though, and it took me too long to get free.

Finally, I broke through the last of the tendrils holding me in place and raced after the witch, telling Chip to stay with the kids. The ghosts didn't seem to be malevolent spirits judging from the little bit of conversation I'd overheard. Cassie was the greatest threat. I had to catch up to her and find out who'd sent her. She couldn't be doing this on her own. One of the other Fae houses had to be behind the plot to control Sadie.

The branches whipped at my face and shoulders while the briars and underbrush tugged at my jeans. I ran blindly through the woods heading in the same direction the witch had taken.

When I broke out of the woods and into more open ground with a road next to me, I looked around. I realized I couldn't see her ahead of me and I slowed and took stock of my surroundings. I'd run into what looked like an orchard of some sort across the road. There was no sign of Cassie anywhere I looked. I moved across the road and knelt down. I murmured a short Fae charm to help me track prey. It was one of the most ancient Fae magics dating back to our more primitive times. It was also very effective.

In the moonlight, which was almost as bright as day to my eyes, I saw where feet had pressed down the grass in the orchard. They curved off to the left back towards the winding road I'd just crossed.

I cursed. If she got to pavement again it would be much harder to track her. My magic was more powerful in the natural world than the man-made one.

Sure enough, the tracks led right to the edge of the road and disappeared. It took me several long minutes to locate where she'd left the road on the other side and ran back into the woods. At first I thought she might be heading back towards Chip and the kids, but then I realized her prints curved again back towards where we'd entered the trees by the monument.

The realization hit me. The van.

I picked up speed knowing where she was headed. If she got there ahead of me, she'd be long gone, and I'd lose the trail for sure.

My long running strides ate up the distance, racing through the forest on the hunt. Deep inside I reveled in the chase. I was a hunter at heart, even more than a warrior. Racing through the trees like this filled me with a primal energy. A few minutes later, I broke out into the open again.

I turned and gained my bearings. There was the metal cross monument. There was the Firebird. I tracked along the tree line, searching for the van where she'd pulled it into the trees.

I found the tracks, but no van. It was gone, and so was Cassie.

Damn it. Another lead to who was behind this lost and perhaps ready to come back at us a different way. I had to track down this witch in addition to what else needed to be done. I had to impress upon Chip how many ways he'd screwed up his responsibilities. I intended to use this against him. This would allow me take Guardianship of the children from him. Aunt Allura had to agree with me after this debacle.

I picked my way back through the woods until I got to the clearing. The ghosts had left to haunt someplace else on this old battlefield. Chip sat with Sadie's head in his lap. He stroked the little girl's dark hair while he hummed a song in a low voice. The scene would almost be touching if it weren't for the reason we were out here in the first place.

He looked up as I got closer. "She got away?"

"Yes, she got away. She took the minivan, so we'll have to make do getting the kids home without a car seat for Sadie." That was something else I intended to use against Chip.

"Not optimal, but it's late, there shouldn't be much traffic to deal with." He nodded at the baby carrier. "You take Addy. I'll carry her."

He bent over and lifted Sadie in his arms, then climbed to his feet. She barely stirred.

I picked up Addy's carrier. He had slept through the whole thing.

We wedged Addy's carrier behind the Firebird's passenger seat and then I got a blanket from the trunk and spread it out on the narrow rear seat for Sadie to sit beside her brother. She lay down and nestled in, falling back to sleep.

"It's not the best but we can get new car seats tomorrow," Chip said as he got in the car and waited for me to start it.

I didn't say anything, instead pulling out slowly onto the country road, heading back home. With the kids in the car, I couldn't yell at Chip about how tonight was all his fault. So, I spent the first few minutes thinking of all the arguments I'd use against him.

He broke the uneasy silence after several minutes. "So, ghosts are a thing. They seemed to hold the Fae in some regard, judging from the brief conversation I had with them."

"They were likely Irishmen, or first-generation descendants of them. People from that land have long had a knowledge of us and our place in the world. It hasn't always been peaceful, for either side, but that had changed by the time of the war. You were lucky those were the ghosts she chose to use for her spell. If it had been another group of the uneasy dead, the outcome could have been much worse. There are many restless spirits who'd have no qualms about helping put a spell on a little Fae girl."

"Look, I know I'm at fault for what happened tonight. But it all worked out, right?"

I glanced his way, my eyebrows raised high in shock at his cavalier response. "You think it's all okay because we got the kids back in one piece? All of this that happened can't be covered with a simple I'm sorry."

I realized I'd started raising my voice when Sadie shifted a little in the back seat. I lowered my tone before continuing. "This is exactly why you're completely unsuited to being their Guardian, Chip. You have no respect for the dangers of the Unusual world and what could happen to these kids."

"It's not like you stuck around to help me learn anything. I've learned more from Bernard the bed troll than you about things I might have to face. You've been setting me up to fail from the very beginning."

I hissed at him in response. "You aren't weaseling out of this and making it my fault. I told you what you needed to do. I even told you no babysitters, but you had to take your girlfriend out for the night. You had to prove you could keep your high-dollar job and still play kingmaker with your money and funds."

He started to respond but stopped when Sadie woke up a little and whimpered in the back seat.

"This isn't over," I whispered. "We'll finish it at home."

He sat back in his seat, staring straight forward as I drove the rest of the way home in silence.

When we got there, he took Sadie up to put her to bed. I settled Addy down again after changing his diaper. It took me singing a Fae lullaby to him to get him back to sleep, one guaranteed to sooth a child with the crooning nature of its soft magic.

When I got back downstairs, Chip and Mia were talking.

"I'm sorry, dearest. You should go up to bed. Rose and I have some things to discuss."

Mia pulled out her phone and checked it. "I suppose I can get a few hours of sleep before I have to catch the shuttle back to the airport. My flight doesn't leave for New York until ten tomorrow. Good night, love. Don't be too long." She leaned in to drop a long kiss on Chip's lips before she sauntered past me at the bottom of the stairs.

She stopped long enough to say, "Good night, Rose. I'm glad the kids are okay. He's trying. He really is."

Trying isn't enough, I thought to myself. Still, I forced myself to be polite to her. "Goodnight, Mia. I won't be here in the morning so have a safe flight."

Her look told me she didn't think I meant it. Maybe she was right. I wasn't in the mood to do more than follow the minimum of good manners.

I waited until I heard the door shut to the master bedroom, then I whirled around to face Chip.

He held up his hands. "Before you lay into me, I'd like to stipulate that everything you're about to accuse me of is the truth."

"You're not getting off that easy, Chip. I'm going to see you get your ultimate wish. I'm going to my aunt and getting her to revoke your Guardianship. I think tonight's episode has proven you're not fit for the job."

"Do what you think you have to, but I'll fight it. I've proven I can protect them, even when I screw up. I might need a little more help along the way, but that's something I'll work out in tandem with you and your aunt. I won't give up the kids, Rose. No way, no how."

I didn't want to say anything else to him. My arguments weren't for him. I saved my words for what I'd say to Aunt Allura when I saw her. She'd know what to do and she'd have to back me on this after tonight.

"I'm going, Chip. I don't have anything else to say to you. Enjoy one of your last nights with the kids. Things are going to change. I'll see to that."

I left him standing there in the middle of the living room and went out to my car. I wanted to scream as I pulled away from the curb. Everything about him made me feel this way. There wasn't anyone else who had this effect on me and lived to do it again. Too bad I couldn't just kill him like all the other adversaries I'd encountered.

It was too late to take things to Allura tonight. I'd call her and set up a lunch for sometime in the next few days and tell her the whole sordid tale. She would have to change her mind and make it so I could have Sadie and Addy back in my care where they belonged. Then I could begin to make up for my failure to protect my sister the way I was supposed to.

20

Chip

I stared at the door after Rose stormed out. The thing that irked me the most about everything she said was she was right. I prided myself at excelling at the things I put my mind to. I'd believed I could apply that same direction of purpose to fitting the kids into my new life down here in Maryland.

I'd failed.

That realization stung. It also brought another thing into focus for me. I loved Sadie and Addison more than I'd ever known. Tonight, though I was frightened. It wasn't for my own safety, but for theirs. The thought of losing them tugged at my heart.

That was alien to me.

I'd always loved the kids in my own way, mostly from afar, or during the occasional visit from Uncle Chip for birthdays and holiday gatherings. That had all changed with receiving the Guardianship over them. I hadn't just gained magical powers and abilities. I'd gained a strong personal bond with the two of them. That bond grew in strength after I'd spent all day and night for the last week and a half with them.

I was pretty sure it wasn't the result of any magical influence either. I'd learned the magical side of this Guardian thing felt a certain way.

This newfound intensity of my feelings had grown on its own, and now that it was there, I couldn't conceive of losing them to anyone or anything. That included Rose.

Rose might love them as much as I did, maybe even more. I didn't know. One thing was certain. I was the Guardian, not anyone else. I'd fight to keep Sadie and Addison safe alongside me, even if I had to give up every other thing in my life that had defined me before.

That thought stopped me in my tracks. I meant it. I'd give it all up to stay with them. Whether it was the fame, the excitement, the New York parties, or the huge fund launches, I'd leave it all behind for them.

Mia came to mind right away as the realization of what I would lose sunk in. She'd made the effort to come down here and be with me when she could, but that was under the unspoken understanding that I'd be returning to New York before long. If I left that all behind, I knew it meant leaving her, too.

Rose thought Mia was just another passing fancy, another super-model to grace my arm at black tie events in the city. Maybe in the beginning that had been so. Over the last six months, though, she'd become so much more. Eddie had even remarked how much we acted like a real couple most of the time. Now it was time to say goodbye and that hurt even thinking about.

She'd offer to keep up the long-distance thing for a while. We both had the money to make traveling between New York and Maryland almost painless. After all, we'd made do when she had trips overseas for weeks at a time. I'd jet away to Paris, or Berlin, or Madrid to see her for a few days then come back to the Big Apple to run my business ventures. She was based in New York, and she always came home for us to reunite after her trips abroad. If I stayed down here, it would make it far too complicated to keep going that way. We couldn't main-tain our relationship that way. She deserved more than that.

I sat on the sofa, the only light in the room coming from the lamp on the table beside me. The room around me felt like home, the place where I belonged. It was a sensation I'd never felt, even in one of my three places up north. This was where I was supposed to be. This was where I would stay.

The sofa's comfortable cushions lured me into laying down to rest.

The night's activities had tired me on many levels, including my magical mana tank or whatever it was. All I wanted was to sleep. I resigned to close my eyes for just a few minutes, then I'd go up and join Mia in the master bedroom.

She woke me a few hours later as she came down to leave and catch her shuttle back to the airport. I started a little when she touched my arm.

I sat up and rubbed at my eyes. "What time is it?"

"A little before six. My shuttle will be here soon." She smiled down at me. "You never came up to join me. It's not like you to miss a chance to be together."

All the thoughts from the night before rushed back through my mind and I looked up at Mia, unable to respond for a few seconds.

A sad smile crossed her lips. She knew. "It's okay, my dear. We both are adults. This couldn't last forever, even when we were back in New York. We eventually had to go our own ways."

"I'm sorry, I—"

Mia reached out to lay a finger on my lips, stopping me. "You're about to tell me you're sorry and that the kids need you. You're right. They do. You have to be here, in mind, body, and spirit. I can't compete with that, nor would I want to."

That last part puzzled me. Mia had never impressed me as the totally unselfish type. "You're not angry with me?"

"No, after you became the official guardian for the kids, I kind of figured this was inevitable."

"Why did you come back down here, then?"

She laughed. "Because we're friends, silly. That'll never change. You lost your brother in a horrible accident. I make it a point to always stand by my friends in difficult times. But the time has come for me to step back and let you find your way down here without me. It's all good. I have a two-week gig at a show coming up in Paris. It's a good opportunity for a break, for both of us."

I stood and pulled her into a tight embrace. "Thank you," I whispered. A hint of her perfume washed over me for the last time.

We stepped back from our hug, and she smiled. "I reserve the right to drop in from time to time if I'm in the area. There are shows I could book with the agency down in Baltimore. It would be fun to catch up every now and then. Does that sound good to you?"

"It does. Thank you for understanding all this."

"I grew up in a tight-knit family of my own. I understand the concepts of duty and the things you must do for them. You understand that now, too."

"I do."

Mia's phone buzzed. She glanced at the screen. "The shuttle's out front to pick me up. Time for me to go." She grabbed her overnight bag and walked for the door. "Keep in touch, Chip. Send me pictures of the kids as they grow up. It'll make me happy to see them as you raise them."

The door shut and she was gone. I realized she'd made that as easy as it was because she let go of me first. She ripped off the bandage fast and the sting was fading a little already. I'd miss her, but she was right. We were a couple of convenience and now life had made it inconvenient.

The clock on the mantle chimed six times. The kids would wake up soon. I went to the kitchen to prep everything for pancakes, along with making up the day's bottles for Addy. I'd face Rose's challenge when it came, but until then, I'd do my best to keep the kids safe and sound with a normal routine at home.

21

Rose

I squirmed a little in the chair while I waited in Aunt Allura's front living room. I always felt like a little girl again whenever I was here. Allura had always been a no-nonsense sort of woman. She didn't allow play when Lili and I had visited as kids, and she believed children should be seen and not heard. That impression of how to act in her home and presence had stuck with me much longer than it should have.

Today, though, I intended to meet my aunt as an equal in the family. We both had powerful interests in making sure Sadie grew up strong and capable so she'd be ready to take up her mantle as the new Fae queen. All I had to do was give Aunt Allura the proof that Chip couldn't do that. I'd recount the events of the past few days while I'd been tracking down the weretigers for her. She'd learn what happened when I left Chip alone for just a short time.

Reston, the butler, came in wheeling a metal cart with a silver coffee urn and a full china coffee service. "The mistress will be here shortly. Can I provide you some coffee while you wait?"

"That would be fine. Thank you. I take it cream and two sugars."

He nodded and set about pouring me a cup of coffee, then expertly added a dash of cream from a small pitcher before he dropped in two sugar cubes from a bowl beside it. He set a teaspoon on the saucer next to the cup and set it on the table. After serving me, he moved to stand behind the cart, staring straight ahead.

I wondered if I should try and make conversation with him. As usual, I decided not to. I didn't have much in common with him as far as I knew. He'd been my aunt's butler and chief household servant for as long as I could remember. He was Fae, like the rest of us, and rumor had it his family had served ours for many, many centuries.

That probably meant he had a weapon or two on him and knew how to use it. Fae retainers weren't just there for show. They were supposed to lay down their lives for their liege lords and ladies. I found myself speculating about whether I could take him or not. He was older than me by at least a century. We Fae were long-lived beings. Still, that put him at the beginning of middle age from a human standard. A person in his position would be a formidable warrior.

I was still pondering the possibilities of a sparring match with Reston when my aunt glided into the room. She always made a grand entrance, even in her own home. Her long gown hid her feet and gave any movement she made a fluidity like floating over water. She sat in the large chair across from me.

As soon as she sat, Reston moved to prepare her coffee and set it beside her. She waited until she tasted the brew and nodded in approval before turning her attention to me.

"Good morning, Rose. What is it that brings you here unannounced this morning?"

"It's about the children's safety, Aunt Allura. They're not safe where they are."

Her brow creased in concern. "Has something happened to them? Sadie hasn't been injured, has she?"

I shook my head. "No, not physically at least, but Chip has done things, and made decisions, that put them in grave danger and at greater risk of discovering who they really are."

"What kind of decisions, exactly?" Allura sat ramrod stiff all the time, but she seemed to straighten even more over the accusation leveled at Chip.

I pulled a folded magazine from my bag and handed it to her. I let the picture on the front cover of Business Weekly do the talking for me.

Allura stared at the magazine for a few seconds before setting it on the table beside her and picking up her coffee cup. She took a sip and said, "That is unfortunate, but hardly worth removing him as Guardian. I'm sure you told him the error he made."

"Of course I did, but he put their pictures on the cover of a national publication. Surely that kind of exposure is dangerous to them."

"Human cameras don't capture the Fae qualities very well. Look at the photo with fresh eyes, my dear. You'll see there is nothing in that photograph but a haughty businessman showing off his family. No one else will see anything different."

I stared at her, trying to comprehend how she wasn't as angry as I was. I'd been sure this would start her down the path of taking the kids away from Chip.

Allura knew she hadn't given me the answer I wanted. I could see it by the amused glint in her eyes.

"Was there something else, Rose?"

"Yes, he hired a nanny to help watch them. She was a witch. She kidnapped them at the first opportunity and tried to cast a glamour on Sadie to exert influence over her mind."

"That is concerning. Why didn't you counsel him on how to hire a proper family servant? That is part of your duty to bring him into understanding the Unusual world and the ways of the Fae."

I crossed my arms. "This isn't my fault, Aunt Allura." Her glare had me feeling like a naughty little girl again.

Allura cocked her head to one side. "Isn't it?"

"I told him not to hire anyone. I told him it was his responsibility alone to care for the kids. What else was I supposed to do?"

"You are there to support him, Rose, not supplant him. You have always been one to mix up your duties with your desires. It dates back to your realization that you were second to Lili in the family. You've never let that go. It is something that is unbecoming in an aunt. Look at me. I supported my sister always, giving counsel to her children long after she'd passed from this earth. You are tasked with doing the same, my dear."

"I supported Lili. I still support her and would do anything for Sadie and Addison."

"Even if that means supporting her final wishes?"

I choked back an angry response. My aunt didn't respond well to such outbursts. Chip was Lili's choice. I'd tested him and grudgingly found him acceptable. "Does that mean I have to let him do whatever he wants to do with the children?"

"No, of course not. You can help him see the error of his ways when his choices are poor. Have I not always told you and your sister when I was displeased with some decision you made? Have I not offered alternative options that you have eventually taken, more often than not?"

"You didn't want her to marry Bobby."

"No, but in some matters, not even the best counsel will win out. It is in those moments that you must be most circumspect in how you react and carry on. I came to accept Bobby, even as I worked hard to make sure Lili adhered to Fae traditions in most things despite her human husband."

"So I have to accept Chip in this role, whether I like it or not?"

Aunt Allura didn't answer. She kept her gaze level and waited for me to continue.

"Fine," I said after several awkward seconds of silence. "I'll keep working with him."

She didn't say anything, she just stared at me.

I floundered for something that would convince her I wasn't in the wrong here. "Aunt Allura, it's not like I was going to abandon the children to his care without help if I didn't get the answer I wanted."

My aunt sipped at her coffee before setting the cup down and rising. I stood when she did. When she rose, my audience with her was over as far as the older woman was concerned.

"Do the right thing, dear. Our family's future depends on it." Aunt Allura gave me the slightest hint of a smile and glided from the room in much the same way she entered.

I picked up the cup and finished the remainder of my coffee.

Reston stood by the doorway into the entry hall waiting for me to make my exit. "I'm coming. I'm sure you have important butler things to do."

"Indeed. Have a good day, Miss Rose."

Outside, I sat in my car for several minutes composing myself after the disappointing results of making my request. I didn't want to accept Chip as Guardian of the children, but if what had happened in the last few days didn't change my aunt's mind, nothing would. That meant Chip was here to stay.

It was in that moment that I understood why I was so upset. I'd always assumed I'd be able to get rid of the infuriating brother-in-law at some point. Now I knew I'd have to work with him, and not just now, but for many years to come.

As if on cue, my phone chirped with a message. It was Chip.

Rose, I'm planning a family outing to the state park with the kids. Would you like to come along?

I stared at the message for a long time before I summoned up an answer. This was obviously Chip's way to bury the hatchet and make up with me. Perhaps he even hoped it would convince me not to oppose him with Aunt Allura. Now that my aunt had passed along her wishes, I didn't have a choice.

Of course, Chip didn't know that.

I let the message wait for several minutes while I sat in my car listening to music and working up my answer. The pounding rock bass helped me swallow my pride as I tapped away at the screen.

I'd be happy to come along. When did you want to go?

Tomorrow is Saturday. How about we meet here at 10AM?

Sounds good. See you then.

I was about to put my phone down when Warren called. I answered it right away.

"What's up? I assume you have some news for me."

"Yeah," Warren answered. "I got a call from a friend in the county sheriff's office. They found Lili's van abandoned outside of town. He saw the name on the registration and knew I was working with the family, so he called me about it."

"Is it damaged in any way?"

"I don't know. I'm on my way down to where they found it to check it out."

I needed to get there and see if there was any way of tracking the witch from something she might have left in the car. "Text me the location. I'll meet you there."

"Okay, I'll see you in a little bit." He hung up.

I waited until the location came through. It was close to the kids' house. That told me Cassie was still interested in carrying out her plan somehow. If she'd been smart, she would've driven to another state and disappeared. I wouldn't let her get away again.

I put the car in gear and drove away. Maybe I could catch her before she put a new plot in motion.

22

Chip

On Saturday morning, I searched the house, looking for the very expensive picnic basket I'd given Lili one year for Christmas. It was one I'd seen in a store in New York City. It had all the upscale items needed for a fancy picnic. I thought it would be the perfect gift for my sister-in-law.

After searching for a half hour, I'd almost given up. She must have regifted it to someone else. I couldn't blame her. It wasn't really suitable for a suburban housewife's picnic. It wasn't until I was grabbing some of the kids' laundry from the basement that I noticed the corner of the basket peeking out from under the checkered blanket that had come with it. Everything inside looked just the way it had when I'd given it to her. She'd never used it.

I carried it and the blanket upstairs to the kitchen and set it on the table.

"What's that, Uncle Chip?" Sadie asked when I pulled away the blanket covering the basket.

"It's a picnic basket. I thought we'd go out to the park later with Aunt Rose. Would that be nice?"

"A real picnic?" Sadie bounced on the balls of her feet in excitement.

"Yes, just the four of us. We'll go up to the state park and picnic in the woods."

"Yes, yes, yes!"

"Okay," I said. "Do you want to help me pack it while Addy sits in his chair and watches us?"

Sadie climbed on a chair and stood on it so she could lean over the table and look in the basket as I unpacked it. The basket included fine china plates and sterling silver cutlery. I thought the plates were a bit much, so I pulled out the china and substituted with some of the left-over paper plates from the funeral luncheon. I left the heavy silver knives, spoons, and forks stowed in their slots inside the fabric lining of the basket's lid.

"What else should we put in?"

"Sandwiches."

"Good idea." I pulled some ham and cheese from the fridge, grabbed the loaf of bread and a bottle of mustard, and returned to the table.

With Sadie's help, I assembled three sandwiches. Two with ham, cheese and mustard. One with just ham and cheese because Sadie wrinkled up her nose at the mustard when I asked her if she wanted any.

We placed the three sandwiches in a large plastic baggie and set them in the basket. I pulled a hard plastic cold pack from the freezer and set it in the basket with a pair of bottles for Addy. I added two cans of soda for Rose and me, a cup with a lid and straw for Sadie, and filled a final baggie with potato chips from a large bag on the counter.

Sadie and I admired our handiwork.

"How's it look?" I asked.

"Perfect. Can we leave now?"

"No, we have to wait for Aunt Rose to get here."

"I'm here," Rose said from the door to the dining room.

I didn't say anything about her not knocking or ringing the door-bell. She'd earned the right to come and go like a resident.

"Good," I said. "We just packed up the basket, but if there's anything else you can think of besides the diaper bag, I think we can load up and go."

Rose came over, looked inside and gave a nod of approval. "You'll be happy to hear that they found the minivan. I brought it with me. The car seats are still in it, and it doesn't seem to be damaged."

"Great, it would've been tight in the Tesla or your Firebird with the new car seats I got yesterday." I picked up Addy. "Can you get Sadie and the basket? I'll go and grab his diaper bag."

Rose did as I asked, and soon we were all loaded up and ready to go on our outing. I was a little irked when Rose situated herself in the driver's seat. I didn't say anything, though. This was supposed to be a nice family trip. I didn't need to start it with an argument about something petty like who did the driving.

"Where are we going, or should I choose?" she asked.

"I planned on the Union Mills park area. There are hiking trails Bobby and I used to go on when we were kids with my parents."

"That works. I know the way."

It didn't take us long to get there, just twenty minutes or so. Rose parked in the gravel lot and we got out. Sadie wanted to go running off right away, but I corralled her with a hand.

"Easy does it. I don't even have Addy moved over into his daddy carrier yet."

Rose raised an eyebrow when I pulled out the harness that would allow me to carry Addison on my chest while we walked. "You're actually going to wear that thing?"

"It beats carrying him in my arms the whole time. You can have a turn if you want."

"Nope, I think that's all you. I wouldn't be caught dead in one of those things."

"Suit yourself. You'll have to carry the basket and blanket then."

"Better to look like a picnicker than a dork."

Sadie giggled. "Dork. That's a funny sounding word. Dork, dork, dork."

"Great, you taught her a new word," I said.

"Living with you, she would've learned it soon enough."

"Ha ha, good one." I finished getting Addy situated in the rig on my chest and I pointed at the nearest trail. "After you, Princess."

Both Sadie and Rose answered, "Thank you."

That set me to chuckling as I followed along behind them.

We hiked along for about a half hour, taking our time and letting Sadie explore in the trees beside the trail with her Aunt Rose nearby to keep an eye on her. I marveled at Sadie's ability to seemingly disappear into the natural surroundings. There were times when neither Rose nor I could locate her until we searched carefully.

"I was playing hide and seek. Mommy said it was my superpower."

Rose said, "As long as you come out when we call you, you can keep playing while we walk."

Sadie ran back into the trees to hide again.

"It's uncanny how she can disappear like that."

Rose searched the trees where Sadie had disappeared. "It's a Fae skill. She already has amazing ability for someone so young. Even I have trouble locating her and I'm a trained huntress. It's harmless, though, as long as she comes out when she's called."

We kept playing with her while we walked. Sadie would run ahead a little and hide while we then searched for her near the trail. It passed the time quickly as we hiked along.

After a while, we found a spot where the trees opened up some but still offered shade around the edges.

"This'll do," I said. "We can put the blanket down and have some lunch and spend time exploring here before we head back."

Rose set the basket down and spread out the plaid blanket on the grass. The park service kept this part of the trail mowed regularly so the grass wasn't very long.

"What did you pack for lunch?" Rose flipped open the lid to check inside.

Sadie danced over and looked inside with her. "Ham and cheese sandwiches. I helped make them."

"Oh, you did, did you? I hope they're good."

"Yours isn't," Sadie said, making a face.

"Why not?"

"Because Uncle Chip made me put mustard on it." She wrinkled up her nose like she had at the house. "Mustard is yucky."

Rose laughed. "You know, I used to think the same thing at your age. I kind of like it now." She nodded in my direction. "Uncle Chip made the right call. Which one is mine?"

Sadie dug out one of the sandwiches and handed it to Rose.

While they set out the rest of the things for our lunch, I took Addy out of the carrier and settled him between my crossed legs with his bottle.

Rose handed me a can of soda and the other mustard-contaminated sandwich. Sadie had already started in on half of her sandwich. She'd worked up an appetite running in and around the trees bordering the trail.

I took a bite and looked around at the woods. "You know, before I learned about the existence of the Unusual world, I would've thought if Fae existed at all, they'd be found out in the forest like this."

"You're thinking of Low Fae or what most call fairies. Their womenfolk have wings, and their men mostly work with the land in some way."

"So that makes you, Sadie, and Addison what? High Fae?"

Rose smiled. "Or high elves, or any of a number of other terms used for people like us over the ages. We used to be quite powerful before the humans gained technology that outpaced their need for our natural magics to help them tend their crops and animals. In some places they still hold us in high regard, but our influence is much diminished from what it used to be."

"So, there might be actual fairies around here right now?" I searched the trees around our small clearing.

"The park staff and rangers who watch over this park are probably mostly Low Fae."

"But wouldn't the women's wings kind of stand out in a public situation?"

"They fold up very small and can be concealed easily with clothing. Most humans wouldn't know what to look for."

I scanned the tree line and hoped for a glimpse of a real winged fairy, even if Rose said they'd look normal like me. That was when I spotted Cassie standing beside a tree. Her grin as she stared back at me was anything but friendly.

"Rose."

"Huh?" She asked around a mouthful of her sandwich.

"Cassie is over there."

Rose whipped around and leaped to her feet. She spit the food on the ground. "You've got a lot of nerve showing up here. You should've run away when you had the chance."

Cassie made no move to approach us. She stood where she was as she answered. "I wasn't going to harm the children, you know. It was just a little glamour to use until she'd grown up."

I stood, sliding Addy into his carrier as I did. I snapped the clips holding him in place. "I trusted you, Cassie. Rose is right. You shouldn't have returned."

"When my friends get here, you won't feel so sure of yourself, Chip. Where's the fancy sword, Rose? Forget to bring it with you?"

Rose cursed under her breath then bent down and grabbed the two silver knives from the lid of the picnic basket. They had pointed tips and a sharp, serrated edge, but they couldn't really be called weapons.

Cassie laughed. "That's the best you have? This is going to be easier than I thought."

"They're silver. They'll carve up any hired muscle you brought along just fine."

Realizing I didn't have any weapons either, I looked around for something to use. Not seeing any alternative, I pulled out the two silver forks.

That set Cassie laughing even harder.

Rose glanced back at me. "Really, Chip?"

I shrugged. "Silver is silver, right?"

"Just stay behind me and keep the kids safe."

Behind Cassie, three hulking figures moved from the shadows. The weretigers let out low snarls and sniffed at the air while looking in our direction.

Cassie pointed at the four of us across the clearing. "Bring me the little girl. You can do what you want with the others."

I pulled Sadie around to stand behind me and crouched with my forks at the ready.

Rose didn't wait. She let out a high-pitched, wailing war cry and charged at the tiger men.

The weretigers leaped from the shadows at the forest's edge and ran at Rose. I was sure they'd swarm her under and keep going straight at the rest of us in an instant.

Instead, Rose bounced into the air, executing a flip as she threw one of the silver knives at the nearest attacker.

The weretiger let out a snarling yowl before falling over backward to lay still with a picnic basket knife embedded in one of his eyes.

"Shit," I muttered as Rose landed to square off with the other two.

"You said a bad word."

I glanced down at Sadie. "I'll set up a swear jar when we get home."

While Rose somehow kept the two weretigers busy with her amazing fighting prowess, I searched the trees for Cassie. She'd disappeared right after the three tigers charged.

"Sadie, honey, I want you to stay behind me, okay?"

"Those men are scary, Uncle chip. Is Aunt Rose going to be okay?"

Rose had blood streaming down her left arm from three ragged claw wounds in her shoulder. She kept fighting to keep herself between them and us, though. One of the weretigers had a distinct limp where she'd obviously scored a hit of her own with the remaining knife.

"She's going to be fine."

Movement to my right drew my attention just in time to see Cassie racing in at me to grab Sadie. I used my only trick and pushed out with my mind, using my outstretched hand as a guide.

The invisible wall of force stopped Cassie short barely six feet away from us. She screwed up her face in anger and pushed at the wall with all her own magical energy. I felt my barrier shove back at me with surprising power.

"It's a good spell, Guardian. But you haven't had the years of magical training I have."

"I can stand here all day. Rose will be finished with your friends soon enough."

Another howl of pain punctuated my statement.

"What are you going to do when the rest of them get here?"

Cassie's sneer sent a shiver down my spine. If she had more help,

Rose would be overwhelmed in an instant. Cassie knew I couldn't hold both her and a group of angry weretigers at bay.

"Sadie, honey, it's time to play hide and seek again."

"Now?"

"Yes, you go and run into the woods until you find the best hiding place you can. Go. Right now. I'll come find you in a little bit. Don't come out for anyone but me or Aunt Rose."

"I'm scared, Uncle Chip."

"I won't let anything happen to you. Now, run!"

I pushed at her with me free hand and she finally ran off between the trees, disappearing into the darkness.

"That won't save her. She's just a child."

"You'll see. Or maybe you won't. Rose seems to have bested another of your tigers."

In the clearing, another weretiger lay on the ground, though it had shifted back to its man-form as it died, just like the first one. It looked like Rose had cut open its throat.

The final weretiger was only slightly injured while Rose now limped as the pair moved in a circle facing each other.

Rose called out to me. "Where's Sadie?"

"Playing hide-n-seek."

"Good. You should go, too, Chip. Save Addy before it's too late."

I knew I couldn't outrun one of the weretigers if there were more of them. Sadie's ability to hide would protect her for now. I decided I was better off here where I could see any attack coming.

"Nope. I'll keep Cassie busy until you're ready to deal with her."

Rose grunted something under her breath I didn't quite catch. She kept her attention on the weretiger in front of her.

I focused on holding back Cassie's magic with my own. I could already feel my mind tiring from the exertion. Snarls of rage sounded from the woods behind me. The other shifters working with the witch must be here. I hoped Sadie had found a really good hiding place. She was going to need it.

23

Rose

Chip seemed to be holding off Cassie for the time being, which was good. I had my hands busy with the final weretiger.

I dodged to the right, trying to offer a feint to the remaining shifter. We were both injured, though I was definitely the worse off between us. My left arm was nearly useless. The claws of the first tiger to reach me had dug deep into the muscle in my shoulder and a later raking attack had cut open my left forearm.

Add in the damage to my right knee from a desperate dodge that barely avoided ending with my stomach ripped open, I was tiring. Unfortunately, I likely tore one of the ligaments in my knee when I did it.

The weretiger opposite me had a few shallow wounds from my pitifully small picnic knife. It was sharp enough, sort of, and the point would penetrate for the kill if I could get in close enough. However, that was the big trick. These shifters were bigger than me and had a longer reach than I did. If I was close enough to hurt them, they could definitely hurt me at the same time.

Damn. Why did I leave the sword in the Firebird at the house?

I didn't see Sadie anymore behind Chip.

Without taking my eyes off the man tiger again, I called out, "Where's Sadie?"

"Playing hide-n-seek."

"Good. You should go, too, Chip. Save Addy before it's too late."

"Nope. I'll keep Cassie busy until you're ready to deal with her."

I shook my head and muttered, "Stupid macho bullshit." As much as I wanted to yell at him, though, I wasn't going to second guess him. Our chances of winning this fight were fifty-fifty at best. He'd probably done the right thing. Sadie stood a better chance out there hiding on her own until me or Chip could come and find her.

Of course, to do that, I had to live through the next few minutes against this weretiger and anything else the witch had lurking out there.

Snarls sounded from the woods behind Chip and Cassie, telling me that Cassie's help had arrived. Chip wasn't equipped to deal with two attacks. He was still feeling his way into his Guardian powers at this stage. I knew he had some martial arts training in his background, but it would be almost useless against powerful shifters like these. His training was probably more about taking out a would-be mugger.

The weretiger in front of me feinted to the left and then charged in at me.

I picked up on what he was doing, though. I pushed off with my one good leg and tried to leap over him while I stabbed down with the knife.

It sort of worked.

I managed to stab down and plant the silver knife in the middle of his back as I sailed over him. I didn't stick the landing very well on the other side, though, and my bad knee buckled as I landed.

A scream of pain erupted from my throat as I felt the knee give way. Then I was on my back trying to roll to my feet before the tiger could turn and leap on me.

I got back onto one foot, trying to be ready to take on an attack, but it wasn't coming.

The weretiger lay writhing on the ground, trying to reach the knife handle jutting out from between his furry shoulder blades.

As I watched, the spasms slowed and then stopped. As it died, it shifted back into human form.

I looked up to see where Chip was, just as another weretiger charged out of the woods at him and Addison.

"Chip, look out!"

There was no way I could reach him in time and all his attention seemed to be focused on holding off Cassie with his barrier spell, or whatever it was.

The werecat charged in at him from the side and I was sure he and the baby were done for.

At the last second, though, Chip spun in place, pivoting so the tiger jumped through the empty space where he'd been standing a mere second before.

The weretiger let out a pained yowl. One of the picnic forks was embedded in his eye. That had it completely occupied for the moment.

I limped forward as fast as I could go, yanked the knife from the dead man's back, and threw it end over end at the yowling tiger man's chest.

The silver blade hissed as it sunk in up to the handle, embedding itself at the base of the neck, just above the notch in its collarbone. Its yowling cut off in a gurgling spray of frothy blood. Then it, too, died.

Cassie took advantage of the break in Chip's concentration to pull away from their magical contest of wills and race into the woods. Based on the sounds out there in the leafy green darkness, there had to be at least one more weretiger left.

"Come on," I said. "We need to get to Sadie before Cassie and that other weretiger out there find her."

Chip pointed to my leg as I hobbled past him. "You're injured. You can barely walk, and your arm is next to useless."

I stopped and fixed him with a level stare. "What's the alternative, Chip? Sadie doesn't stand a chance alone out there if they find her first."

"Cassie didn't plan to kill her before. She just wanted to cast a spell on her."

"There's no way she can do that now. We're on to her. The only play is to take out the heir so another can be chosen."

The hesitation was plain in Chip's eyes. It took me a second before I realized what it was. "Chip, you have to get over any chivalrous values you might be carrying around about hitting a girl. Cassie will kill all of us if she gets the chance. Don't think, don't blink, just take her out. Do you understand?"

He opened his mouth to argue his case.

"No, I mean it. The kids' lives depend on you making the right choice here. It's her or them. You are the Guardian, and this is part of the job. Which is it going to be?"

Chip reached up and placed a hand on Addy's chest in the carrier he wore. The screwed-up frown on his face told me he didn't like the decision he had to make, but I also saw determination return to his eyes. "I can do it. Let's get out there."

A roar in the woods punctuated his statement.

"They've found her trail," I said. "Come on. Use your link to Sadie. We can get there first, if we hurry."

Chip stared at the woods for a few seconds then pointed off to the right a little. "That way."

"Let's go." I started in the direction he pointed, letting him take the lead. He could walk faster than I could, and he was the one who could tell where Sadie was. On the way past the dead man on the grass, I retrieved the silver picnic knife.

Chip picked up the pace, and I was hard-pressed to keep up. I didn't want him to slow down, though. We had to get to Sadie. Nothing else mattered.

I stumbled over a rock jutting up in the trail and cursed aloud.

Chip stopped and looked back my way. "You okay, can I help you?"

I pushed his hand away. "No. Keep going. I'll catch up. Find her, Chip. You're the only one who can."

He seemed uncertain about leaving me, then he took off at a faster, jogging pace down the rough wooded trail.

I limped along after him, keeping the best pace I could. Following his trail was no problem. Chip was no trained woodsman. He left a trail a blind Fae could follow.

After about ten minutes of plowing through the forest, I heard Chip call out up ahead. "Sadie, where are you?"

I pushed myself to the last inch of my endurance and pain tolerance until I reached a tall, thick oak tree in the middle of a ring of similar but smaller oaks. Chip stood in the middle of the small clearing with his hand against the big tree.

"What is it, Chip? Have you lost the trail?"

"She was here, but I can't sense her direction from here. I can feel her sort of, but only in a general sense."

"Is she injured?" I worried that Cassie had found her first.

"No, I don't think so." He cocked his head to the side and stared off into the woods. "It's like she's puzzled, curious about something. That's all I'm getting."

I looked around, taking in the ring of oaks. "This is a Dryad's grove. That central tree is the forest fairy's home."

"A Dryad? I don't think I've ever heard of them before. Are they dangerous?"

"Not usually. They look like you and me for the most part, but their affinity for forests and their sacred groves draws them to working in fields involving nature in some way. It's possible she works near the park somewhere."

"She took Sadie? How come I can't feel her direction, then?"

"It's nature magic," I said with a shrug. "Dryads have a set of powers all their own in their home environments. It's possible Sadie told her about the weretigers and she's trying to protect her somehow. She has to know there are shifters and other powerful beings in her forest."

A roar interrupted us. It wasn't that far away, and it was followed by a woman's scream. I didn't need Chip's ability to home in on that.

I pointed. "That way. Come on!"

This time I moved ahead of him, keeping him behind me so Addy stayed safe. There was a fight going on in the woods not far away. Shouts and angry snarls told me that much.

I finally got close enough to see the orange striped fur of the weretiger charging across a clearing ahead. Its target was a woman wearing a forest ranger's uniform with a broad-brimmed cap. Bloody gashes showed through tears in the front of her pale green ranger's shirt. She had taken a fighting stance and prepared to receive the shifter's attack. This was the Dryad.

The pain faded from my mind as I spotted Sadie off to the side, hiding behind a tree. If the weretiger overwhelmed the woman, the little girl was next. Somehow, I willed my injured leg to work, and I pushed off at a hobbled, stumbling run forward.

I tackled the tiger man just as he was about to leap on the ranger. We tumbled and rolled on the ground. I'd taken him by surprise, but that advantage only lasted a few seconds.

I stabbed at him again and again, while I tried my best to keep the clawed hands away from me with my free hand. We rolled to a stop a few feet away.

The heavier shifter got the advantage and rolled on top of me, pressing me down and batting the bloody, silver knife from my hand.

Pinned down, I waited for the long fangs in that tiger mouth to rip out my throat as I struggled in vain beneath him. Then the weight of him was gone and he fell to the ground beside me.

The ranger stood over us, a large, glowing oak cudgel in her hands. She raised the club and swung it down again, striking the weretiger in the face. Golden sparks showered the air as the blow connected.

The weretiger's glowing yellow eyes rolled up in its head and it lay still on the ground.

I rolled onto my side, my hand outstretched and groping for the knife. I found it and gripped the pitiful blade in my hand as I got up to one knee. My bad leg was completely useless at this point, and I wasn't sure I could walk at all.

On my hands and one good knee, I started to crawl to where the bloody, naked man lay in the tall grass nearby. I had to finish him before he healed and woke up. Shifters regenerated wounds that didn't kill them outright.

The ranger stepped into my way. "No. You'll not kill him. I'll make sure he faces the authorities for whatever crimes he's committed. Unless you want the same fate for murder in my forest, I suggest you stand down."

"You saved my niece. She's the one they were after."

"They?" the Dryad ranger asked. "I thought it was just a rogue weretiger after her."

"There were others back at the clearing and there's a witch out there, too." I searched the tree where Sadie had been hiding. She wasn't there anymore. "Where is she? I saw her standing right over there."

"The girl ran off while you and the weretiger fought. I couldn't break away to stop her."

"Chip will find her, then. Now that she's out from under your protection, he should be able to sense her again."

The ranger pulled a pair of hand cuffs from her belt and knelt down to cuff the shifter's hands. "Your niece is lucky I stopped back home to grab lunch today. I usually pack it in my truck while I'm working."

"Let's hope her luck holds. There's still danger out there. It's up to her uncle now."

I stared into the forest where I'd last seen Sadie. Chip had to get to her first. I wouldn't allow my mind to consider any other option.

24

Chip

Rose somehow ran past me on her bum leg and raced ahead towards the fighting. I ran behind with Addy, trying to keep up with her impossible burst of speed. I saw her tackle the weretiger just before it jumped the forest ranger.

I caught a bit of movement from the corner of my eye. Someone off to the right had just run into the woods, but I couldn't see who it was. A second later, the sense of Sadie's direction came back to me. She was in the same direction as the movement I'd seen. It was either her running or someone else chasing after her.

Without a second thought, I raced off into the woods after them. I had to get to Sadie first. There wasn't a trail to walk on this time and briars and other brush did its best to inhibit my chase.

Sadie's frightened shout made me redouble my efforts, trying as best I could to shield Addison from the brush whipping around us. I heard another familiar voice just ahead and my heart wrenched.

Cassie had gotten there first.

"You've caused me no end of trouble, little girl. My mistress wants you to live for now, but I might just tell her you had a horrible accident anyway."

The vitriol that dripped from the witch's voice sent a shiver down my spine. I shouted, "I'm coming, Sadie. Hold on!"

Sadie's sobbing cries reached me as I plowed through the undergrowth and barreled into the opening in the forest where Sadie had fallen beside a large boulder. Cassie stood on the opposite side of the small space.

The witch sneered at me as I ran from cover and stopped beside Sadie, facing the danger.

"I'll finish you all in one go, then." She raised her arms up and I saw purple lightning crackle from her fingertips.

My hand extended and I pushed with my will as I'd learned to do, throwing up a barrier against whatever spell was coming. Unfortunately, I placed the barrier in the wrong place.

A blast of magical lightning lanced down from above, striking me in the shoulder. It blasted me aside with the energy of a speeding car striking me.

I reached out with one hand to break my fall so I wouldn't land on Addy. The bones snapped just above my wrist as the full weight of my body came down on my extended arm.

Through the haze of pain, with a crying baby strapped to my chest, I got back to my feet just in time to throw my will in between Cassie's next strike and her intended target. This one was aimed at Sadie.

The next bolt of lightning lanced down straight at my niece.

On a last-second impulse, I tried to angle my invisible shield. If I could set it just right, I could…

The purple bolt of magical energy struck the barrier just inches above Sadie's head. The force of the impact drew so much of my mana energy, it buckled my legs until I landed on my knees.

My plan worked, though. The angle of the shield bounced the purple lightning outward.

It flowed off the shield straight at the witch who'd called it down from above, striking Cassie in the chest and flinging her backward. She slammed into a tree before sliding down the trunk and slumping to the ground.

"Sadie," I gasped through gritted teeth. "Are you okay?"

"Uh-huh."

Cassie groaned and started to rise.

"Quick, honey, get behind the boulder." I pointed at the large rock behind the little girl while I staggered over to place myself between her and Cassie.

Blood trickled down from Cassie's nose and ears. I wondered if I looked as bad.

I forced myself to laugh at her. "Hurts, doesn't it."

She didn't respond. All she did was shake her head a little to clear her still foggy mind.

I took a few steps in her direction, trying to decide what to do next.

Cassie still looked disoriented, so I kept coming towards her until I was right in front of her. Rose's words came to mind, and I remembered the lightning coming down straight at Sadie.

In the end, it was easier than I expected it to be. I balled up my fist and sent an uppercut straight into Cassie's chin, snapping her head back and sending her crashing back to the ground.

I stood over her, making sure she stayed down. I didn't have to worry. She was out for the count.

Something small hit me from behind, right at the knees, as Sadie ran out from her hiding place and wrapped her tiny arms around my legs. Her sobbing interrupting her words.

"Uncle <sniff> Chip <sniff> I'm scared. Is <sniff> she asleep?"

I knelt down and placed my good arm around her shoulders. "Yes, honey. She's sleeping and I'm going to make sure she never bothers you again."

Sadie squeezed me back in response.

Unsure what to do, I decided to take Sadie back through the woods towards where I thought Rose and the park ranger were located. With one arm broken, I couldn't do anything to restrain Cassie if she did wake up. I had to make sure Sadie was nowhere nearby when that happened. Rose would know what to do with the witch.

The whole left side of my body ached and tingled. I figured it was a result of taking the magical lightning blast. I hoped it would wear off. I didn't want to think about feeling like this forever. Thank goodness

Addison seemed to be fine. He fussed a little now, but I was able to calm him by bouncing him a little in the carrier.

"Come on, kiddo. Let's go and find Aunt Rose."

"And Miss Kendra?"

"Who's Miss Kendra?"

"The lady with the big hat." Sadie put her arms up around her head in a big circle.

"You must mean the park ranger I saw. Yes, let's go and find Miss Kendra, too."

Together, with Sadie clutching my good hand with both of hers, we walked back through the woods. I tried to make shushing sounds to sooth Addison's fussing. He wasn't really crying, just complaining. Who could blame him?

I heard voices ahead and angled my way towards them. I reached the open spot where Rose sat on the ground with her injured leg stretched out in front of her. The park ranger stood next to her. They both looked our way as we emerged from the undergrowth.

"You must be Kendra," I said as I led Sadie forward. "Thank you for saving my niece."

"This is my forest. They've got a lot of nerve coming in here and attacking people on my turf."

"We're probably better off that they did. We might not have survived otherwise, right Rose?"

"If I'd had my sword, things would've turned out differently. I'd say we didn't do bad considering our only weapons were picnic basket knives."

Kendra laughed. "I wondered where you'd come up with the strange silver weapons. That must be some fancy picnic basket."

Rose nodded in my direction. "Blame him. There's no way my sister bought that thing. You must have given it to them as one of your overpriced and useless gifts."

Ignoring the slight, I said, "Aren't you glad I did? It all turned out in the end."

"Where's the witch?" Rose asked.

"I left her back there. I knocked her unconscious, but I had no way to tie her up with my arm broken."

Kendra looked around, taking stock of the situation and our location. She dug into her pocket and pulled out her cell phone. "You two stay put. I'm calling in backup and an ambulance for the two of you." She started to dial a number as she walked back the way I had come.

"Where are you going?" I asked.

"I have to find that witch you knocked out. If she's still alive, we're going to have questions for her. If not, we'll have even more questions for you."

I waited until the ranger left us alone then sat down on the grass next to Rose. "Look at us, Rosie. Aren't we a pair?"

"I've told you not to call me that."

"Aw, come on. This is a special occasion. We survived our first fight, and it wasn't even with each other." I smiled and leaned over to nudge her with my shoulder.

She chuckled. "I suppose you're right. Infuriating, but right."

Sadie came over and snuggled in between us before pulling us both in close to her with her little arms. We sat like that, enjoying the quiet for a few minutes.

Kendra came back just as a few groans started coming from the restrained shifter lying on the grass nearby.

"Hey, he's waking up," Rose warned. "Someone should knock him out again. He'll rip apart those cuffs without any trouble."

Kendra shook her head. "Not my cuffs. They're made of a special silver alloy. This isn't my first time locking up a shifter in my park. He won't be getting out of those handcuffs any time soon. Help is on the way." She turned her sharp gaze on me. "Did you have to slit the witch's throat?"

"What? She was just knocked unconscious. I swear!" I struggled to think of an excuse to defend myself. Then I wondered who'd come along and killed Cassie after I'd left.

Kendra stood and stared down at me for a few seconds. "You could be telling the truth. I don't see any blood on you but what looks like your own. I imagine whoever did that would have a good bit more on them. Still, we'll need a statement and have to do some DNA blood swabs to confirm what you're saying."

Her phone chirped and she moved away to talk to whoever had called her.

I leaned close to Rose. "Who else is out there on our side that would've killed Cassie like that?"

"You're assuming they were on our side. Maybe they didn't want Cassie talking to the authorities about who hired her."

I thought about it. "She did mention something about her mistress at one point. Does that mean someone else was controlling her?"

"Or hired her to do a specific job. Now they're cleaning up the mess so no one knows how to follow the trail higher."

"So, we need to worry about more attacks?" I asked. "I'm not sure I can handle any more right now."

"Me neither," Rose said. "Still, maybe this was the big play and it failed. It might mean they'll back off for a bit. We'll have to see. I've got some assets I can call in to back us up at the house if we need it until you and I heal up. We might even want to hire some normal security types to help from your side of things, too, if you're willing. I only have a few in the Unusual community I'd trust with taking up the fight for us."

"I have a top-notch guy who'd come running if I ask him to. He's an ex-Army Special Forces type and he's not cheap, but he'd be able to do the job and do it in a way that didn't call extra attention to us."

"That would be good. The kids don't need the extra excitement messing up their routine. The last few days have been more than enough."

We both pulled out our phones and started sending a few quick messages while we waited for the ambulance and park police to arrive. It didn't take them too much longer to find us in the woods with Kendra's help. They brought four-wheelers along so we didn't have to walk back to the parking lot. Once we got there, they loaded us all right into the waiting ambulance.

Kendra poked her head in before the paramedics loaded up their gear to leave. "Hey, I'll have one of my colleagues come down to the ER to take your statements and make sure the hospital collects any evidence we need. They found the other bodies in the clearing where you said. I don't think you'll be in any further legal trouble. Things match with your story so far. But be prepared to answer a lot of questions. This many bodies draws a lot of unwanted attention."

She waved and backed away as the paramedic climbed in the back with all of us and pulled the door closed. I winced a little as the unit bounced along in the gravel lot until it hit smoother pavement. My broken arm throbbed and had started to swell around my wrist. The paramedic had given me an ice pack and fashioned a sling for me to secure it on the way to the hospital.

He and his partner had splinted Rose's leg and bandaged her clawed-up arm. She sat back on the stretcher while I sat on the bench seat, Addison still strapped to my chest. Sadie rode in a car seat they'd pulled out of a side compartment just for kids her age.

Soon we were on even highway pavement and heading to the hospital. I realized we'd left our lunch and the picnic basket behind. We could always buy another, if we ever decided to picnic again. I think we'd wait a while until things settled down and everyone was healed. I couldn't handle another picnic right now, even if I wanted to.

I settled Addy in his carrier on my chest. The smooth rocking of the ambulance had put him back to sleep. It threatened to do the same with me, even with the pain in my arm. The magical energy I'd expended had exhausted me. All I wanted to do was rest now we were all safe.

25

Rose

The buzzer rang. Someone was down at the front door to my apartment building. I hobbled in my leg brace over to the intercom panel by the apartment door.

"Yeah?"

"It's me, Warren."

"Come on up." I pressed the door release button for a count of two and then unlatched my apartment door, leaving it partially open so he could let himself in when he got up to my floor.

He got there just as I eased myself back down into the chair and lifted my leg back up on the ottoman to elevate it on the pillow there.

"Rose?" He called from the hallway.

"Come in. It's open."

Warren poked his head in the doorway to look around and then came in, shutting the door behind him. "You look better than the last time I saw you."

"It's been a week, Warren. I should hope I look better than I did when you came to see me in the ER."

"I see the leg's still in the brace." He pointed at my arm in the sling. "What about that? Any permanent damage?"

"I'll heal. I don't have a shifter's ability to regenerate, but I heal faster and more completely than a human would."

"Speaking of humans, how's Chip?"

I frowned. "I haven't talked with him since yesterday. He seems well enough. I don't think he'd tell me the truth even if he was doing badly."

"At least the docs said he had a pretty clean break."

"That's still four to six weeks in a cast for a normal person," I said. "I'll be up and out of this brace this time next week."

Warren laughed. "You always were a hardheaded woman, Rose. By the way, I've stopped by the house several times to check on the security we set up there. Chip seems to be getting on well enough. The two neighborhood ladies from across the street have pitched in to help him during the daytime."

"They haven't spotted your people, have they?"

"No, I have a friend in the county public works department. He loaned me a van out of the motor pool and some uniforms. We've got the manhole cover pulled just outside the house and have been pretending to do work there."

My eyebrows shot up. "You've been there a week and no one is suspicious that you haven't finished the work yet?"

"A few people have stopped by the van to ask about it. My guys told them they're calibrating the water and sewer pressure levels as part of a federal study. They all just nod and walk away." He chuckled. "A few have even brought them out refreshments. Gotta love the suburbs."

"As long as no one knows what they're really doing there," I said. "I want to make sure there's protection on the house until I'm back on my feet."

"No one's getting in there past my team. I handpicked them." He paused and pulled out his phone. "Which brings me to the other reason I came by." He tapped the screen a few times and I heard the distinctive swoosh of an email being sent.

My phone buzzed a second later. "What did you just send me?" I picked up my phone from the side table to check.

"That's the coroner's and police report on one Cassidy Reed. It's been ruled a homicide, but it looks like Chip is in the clear. None of the blood on him matches hers. All the other bodies in the woods have been called self-defense and chalked up to a crystal meth gang gone crazy."

I scrolled through the report he sent me. "Any evidence of who did kill her? There had to be someone else out there in the woods who did it."

Warren shrugged. "If anyone knows, it didn't get into either report. Her throat was cut by a long smooth-edged blade. Could be a dagger or even a sword."

"So, we don't know who else is out there waiting to attack?"

"If I were a betting man, I'd say whoever it is has cut and run to regroup. They have to know our guard is up and we beat the best they had to send. Weretigers are no joke and not cheap to hire. Whoever it was had to spend a pretty penny to get them to do this. I'm guessing they're stepping back to wait for things to settle down some."

"Then we'll have to keep the pressure up. That way we let them know we're not letting our guard down."

"I can't keep that van there for too much longer, Rose. We either have to get Chip to let us put someone in the house or you have to come up with a way to protect them from a distance."

"I have a few ideas, but they'll have to wait until I get closer to full strength. Can you hold the van there for another week?"

Warren shook his head. "Five more days is all you have. I have to return it this coming Friday by the end of the workday. After that, someone will notice it's gone, and my buddy won't be able to cover for it anymore."

I rubbed at my messed-up knee through the brace. "Five days will have to do the trick then."

Warren winced and said, "Give me a few days to see if I can come up with something else to try out."

"No, I've already asked you to extend your favors far enough. Aunt Allura has a lot of money, but eventually, she's going to question where all of it's going after I'm up and around again."

Warren seemed to accept my explanation easily enough which told me I was right about him being overextended in the favor department.

"Hey, thank you," I said to him. "I mean it. The family owes you one, big time."

He swept a hand from his head down to his waist as he bowed low in a grand gesture of a past time. "I'm a loyal retainer of the royal family line. My service is the least I can do."

"Oh, stop it. Save it for my aunt. She lives for that shit."

Warren started for the door. "Can I get you anything while I'm here?"

"I'm good. Thanks for bringing the information. I'll be up and around before you have to pull out your security team."

He waved goodbye and let himself out.

I started reading through the police and coroner's reports again, trying to see if there was any clue that might point me at who had set this whole attack in motion. There had to be a key that tied it all together.

After spending an hour pouring over the documents and looking back at the information from Lili and Bobby's deaths, I still had no clues that linked the two crimes or pointed at the person behind it all. I knew in my heart there was someone trying to take out my family. With Cassie's demise, however, the final link that might have tied back to a hidden figure working in the background was gone.

Warren might be right. He was good at his job. He had instincts I had learned to trust. If he thought whoever was behind this was pulling back to regroup, maybe that was the case. It didn't mean Chip and I could afford to let our guards down. But perhaps we could afford to take a deep breath, heal up, and try to settle into a routine that protected Sadie and Addison. They deserved a return to some sort of normal so they could get on with growing up.

I set the phone aside, putting all the reports out of my mind. I needed to heal up and that meant focusing on helping my body knit its broken parts back together. If I turned inward and engaged in meditation to enable my inner Fae full access to power, I could definitely be well enough to take over the security for the kids again.

My eyes closed as I lay my head back on the recliner, I drifted into a deep state of peaceful rest and let the magic do its work.

26

Chip

I shook my head and repeated myself again. "No, Eddie, I can't come up to New York. I have to stay down here in Maryland for the foreseeable future. You'll have to take over the reins and run the launch yourself."

"Come on, Chip. You've been through tough times before. Just get another babysitter and come up here. We need you. It won't be the same without Chipster at the helm."

"I don't think you understand, Eddie. I had my lawyer draw up some documents. I've signed them and they'll be filed with the SEC. I've divested myself completely from the fund. I sent the documents to legal this morning. I'm done. I'm needed down here."

"Chip." Eddie drew out my first name in a cajoling tone. "Chipster. Come on. This isn't the man who bested all the other fund managers in New York last year. I know better."

"No, Eddie, you don't. I'll be watching to see how you do. It's your turn to shine. Go and do it." Sadie walked into the kitchen from the family room, and I held up a finger to tell her to wait. "I have to go now, Eddie. You have a good time up there for me."

I disconnected the call and smiled at Sadie. "What do you need, sweetie?"

"The funny wolf men working in the street are leaving."

I chuckled at her imagination. "Are they now? Well, I'm glad they're done working on whatever it was they were doing. I don't relish the thought of having a problem with the pipes cutting off our water supply."

I followed her back into the front of the house. She led me to the window and pointed.

"See, they're leaving."

"Well, they have other jobs to go to." I saw them packing up their orange road work signs and stacking them on the rack on top of the white van. Their county public services uniforms and high-vis yellow vests marked them as the real deal.

I let the curtain fall back across the window, noting the new electronic sensors on the window my friend Derek had installed with his security team after we returned home from the hospital two weeks before. It was the best system money could buy.

Ellie and Barb had been over helping with meals and things. The two women had filled him in on the long-term utility work happening out front. The pair were better than any website or news channel. They were plugged into anything that happened in the neighborhood.

My phone buzzed in my pocket. I pulled it from where I stowed it in my sling with my good hand. It was Rose.

"Hey, Rose. What's up?"

"I'm on my way over. I wanted to help you out a little and go over what we needed to do moving forward."

"Are you sure you're okay? I'm fine here on my own." She'd called to check in every couple of days since the incident in the woods, but I knew she'd had severe, life-threatening injuries of her own to deal with.

"I'm Fae, Chip. I heal faster than you do. I'm mostly fine."

"Okay, come on over. Honestly, I could use someone here besides the soccer moms. Between Ellie and her trying to mother me all the time, and Barb constantly trying to stay overnight, I would enjoy just having family around."

"What?" Rose said. Her mocking tone said it all. "Is the studly Chip Proctor out to pasture now? Surely a hot soccer mom isn't too much for you to handle."

"Ha ha, Rose. I'm trying to build a home here for the kids. They don't need me rotating women in and out of their lives. They need something stable and regular for a while."

"That's one of the reasons I'm coming over. I have some news about the whole situation to chat about."

"How soon will you get here? Addison will be up from his nap shortly."

"I'm only a few minutes away. We can talk before he wakes up or after. It won't take long."

"Good enough. See you when you get here."

I cut off the phone. "Good news, Sadie. Aunt Rose is on her way over."

"She is?" Sadie clapped her hands. "I miss her so much."

"I do, too." It was one of those automatic answers you gave kids, but as soon as I said it, I knew it was the truth. As much as she annoyed the crap out of me sometimes, we'd made a good team keeping the kids safe out there in the woods. It had opened my eyes to how much I had to learn about this strange Unusual world I'd become a part of.

Rose hadn't been by to see me and the kids since her injuries had sidelined her. I couldn't blame her. She'd nearly died fighting to protect Sadie, Addison, and myself and I'd thought it would take a long time for her to heal. Based on her call, though, I guess I was wrong.

A few minutes later, Rose let herself in the front door. Sadie ran across the room and leaped up into her aunt's arms. She hardly showed any sign of the injuries she'd sustained a few weeks before.

"Aunt Rose, did you see the silly wolf men working out front? Uncle Chip doesn't believe me."

Rose's eyebrows shot up and she looked out front at the workers cleaning up their site in front of the house. She glanced my way and nodded at Sadie. "How long has this been going on?"

I shrugged. "Pretty much since the workers got here. She's got quite the imagination. I went out to check with them on the first day. They were happy to show me their paperwork. They're really a county utility crew. Ellie and Barb confirmed it. They're plugged in to everything around here."

"Well," Rose said with a chuckle. "If Ellie and Barb said it's on the up and up, I won't disagree with them."

I figured that was it until I saw a strange look she gave Sadie as the little girl went back into the family room to grab something to show her aunt. I shrugged. Maybe it was just my imagination.

We spent a few minutes giving Sadie the attention she craved from her aunt. Eventually, she settled into playing by herself and Rose gestured for me to join her in the dining room by the kitchen door.

"So, what's the deal with everything? Did you track down the mastermind behind what happened to Lili and Bobby?"

Rose shook her head. "No, and Warren and I turned over every rock we could think of. He's decided whoever they are, they've pulled back to regroup and reassess things. After looking over everything he's found, I'm inclined to agree."

"So that's it? It's over?"

"That's why I came here. I wanted to ask you. What do your Guardian senses tell you?"

"You're asking my advice?" I didn't bother to hide my shock at her question.

"Look, we worked well as a team out there. I want to include you in any decisions that affect the kids. Do you have any inkling of trouble? It could be a strange feeling, or bad dreams. Anything?"

I thought about it and after a few seconds, I shook my head. "Honestly, aside from my broken arm and dealing with trying to make do with one hand most of the time, things are pretty much back to some semblance of normal."

"Then I think Warren is right. It doesn't mean we let our guards down, but I think we can reset things a little and try and come up with a system that'll let us provide for their safety while raising them."

I raised one eyebrow in question at what she said. "Are you proposing a partnership, Rose?"

"I am. I won't lie, Chip. You screwed up hiring Cassie and inviting her into this house. That gave her power over you and the kids using her magic. It was an unnecessary risk."

I started to interrupt her to defend myself, but she held up a hand to stop me.

"But it's my fault that I didn't fully explain the risks to you when I told you not to do it. We can do a lot more working together than apart. I want to help you be the best Guardian you can be."

Her words shocked me. This was a different side of Rose. It wasn't the hard-nosed sister-in-law I'd alienated all those years ago after our tryst in the coat closet at Lili and Bobby's wedding. Maybe this was her way of burying the hatchet.

"I'm game if you are. I could use the help. What did you have in mind?"

"I'll keep investigating Lili and Bobby's deaths on the side. I'll keep you in the loop on what I find. When I'm in town, I'll help you out with the kids so you can get a break when you need it. You can even get away to go back to New York if you have to."

"I won't have to do that anymore. I cut my ties to the fund launch and the rest of my business ventures up there. The kids were too important and there was no way I could do both." My hand drifted up to my shark's tooth pendant. It was my reminder that I could be useful here influencing these two little kids, just like I'd influenced my brother growing up.

Rose smiled. "I like hearing that. I'm sure it'll make the kids happy, too. So, what can I do to help out? I figure I'd stay here during the day as much as you need me."

Addison started crying upstairs. His voice came over the baby monitor sitting on the table in the dining room.

She laughed. "I guess that's my answer. I'll go and get Addy up from his nap. Then I'll come down and help you with dinner, okay?"

"Works for me."

Rose headed upstairs for the baby. I watched Sadie playing with her toys in the corner. I knew I could do this on my own if I had to, but something about knowing Rose would be around felt right some-how. I smiled and went into the kitchen to get dinner started. This newfound family of mine would be hungry soon.

The End

Read the exclusive story **Guardian's Test** when Rose first tests Chip to become Sadie's Guardian, and join Jamie Davis' email newsletter.

Get the next book, *Fae PTA,*
book 2 in Uncle Chip Saves the Fae

Afterword

Author's Note: May 10, 2024 — It's rainy day here in Maryland a few days before the release of *Unlikely Guardian*. I'm wrapping up some final details of the book's launch next week. I realized I needed to write a message to the readers who might be interested enough to read through to this page after the end of the story.

So, first and foremost, thank you! You're here and that in and of itself is super special to me. Thanks for reading the book. With every book, my hope is that you, the reader, enjoy your time immersed in the story. This one is a little different. There's a little bit more of me inside these pages than usual because Uncle Chip is me.

No, I wasn't a Wall Street fund manager who dated super models once upon a time. My wife would have a good laugh at that one. No, that wasn't me. But I was a dad who gave up a successful career to stay home full-time with my kids. I went through a lot of the mundane parenting moments as a stay-at-home dad in the 90s and early 2000s at a time when it wasn't something most men did. It was important because for me, family comes first. Every. Single. Time.

I've always been one who could buck a trend with the best of them. I didn't mind hanging at the bus stop with the other at-home parents (almost always moms). I ran my three kids to their soccer and swim team practices, and did all the things to raise my family. I did once speculate that if little girls were made of sugar and spice and everything nice, why did their poop smell so bad. Ha ha ha.

I'm looking forward to carrying this story forward and watching Sadie grow up to become the Queen of the Fae she's destined to be. Next up, is the story of Sadie starting first grade a few years after the story in this book. I hope you'll stick around and see what shenanigans ensue in Fae PTA. Maybe Rose and Chip will finally get over themselves and really work together to protect the kids. We shall see.

If you're still reading here and want to learn more about Chip and Rose's origins together, check out the short story, *Guardian's Test*. Just enter your email when prompted to join my email newsletter and read the story of Rose testing Chip at the request of her sister, Lili.

See you again soon at the end of *Fae PTA*. I'll check in again there. In the meantime, stay safe out there.

Jamie

Also by Jamie Davis

Get a free book and updates for new books.
visit JamieDavisBooks.com/send-free-book/

Extreme Medical Services Series

(A 9-book Urban Fantasy series starting with)

Book 1 - Extreme Medical Services

—

Eldara Sister Series

The Nightingale's Angel

Blue and Gray Angel

—

Uncle Chip Saves the Fae Series

(An Urban Fantasy Romp Set it the Extreme Medical Universe)

Book 1 - Unlikely Guardian

—

Lone Wolf Squadron Series

(a 9-book Space Western series starting with)

Marshal the Stars

—

The Huntress Clan Saga

(A 6-book Urban Fantasy series starting with)

Huntress Initiate

—

The Broken Throne Series

(A 5-Book Dystopian Urban Fantasy
starting with)

The Charm Runner

—

The Accidental Traveler LitRPG Series

(with C.J. Davis)

(A 6-book Epic Fantasy Series starting with)

The Accidental Thief

—

Follow on Facebook for updates, news, and upcoming book excerpts

Jamie's Fun Fantasy Readers Facebook Group

Help the Author

I Need Your Help ...

Without reviews indie books like this one are almost impossible to market.

Leaving a review will only take a minute — it doesn't have to be long or involved, just a sentence or two that tells people what you liked about the book, to help other readers know why they might like it, too. It also helps me write more of what you love.

The truth is, VERY few readers leave reviews. Please help me out by being the exception.

Thank you in advance!

Jamie Davis

About the Author

Jamie Davis, RN, NRP, B.A., A.S., is a nationally recognized medical educator who began educating new emergency responders as a training officer for his local EMS program. As a media producer, he has been recognized for the <u>MedicCast Podcast</u> (<u>MedicCast.com/blog</u>), a weekly program for emergency medical providers like EMTs and paramedics, and the Nursing Show, a similar program for nurses and nursing students. His programs and resources have been downloaded over 6 million times by listeners and viewers.

Jamie lives and writes at his home in Maryland. He lives in the woods with his wife, three children, and a dog.

Follow Jamie Online
www.jamiedavisbooks.com

www.ingramcontent.com/pod-product-compliance
Lightning Source LLC
Chambersburg PA
CBHW021710190726
48289CB00008B/2467